THE NATIVES
OF HEMSÖ

THE NATIVES
OF HEMSÖ
by
AUGUST
STRINDBERG

———✦———

Translated from the Swedish

by

ARVID PAULSON

———✦———

Introduction by
RICHARD B. VOWLES

Published for
The American-Scandinavian Foundation
by
PAUL S. ERIKSSON, INC.
New York

*This translation is dedicated
to the memory of
Dudley Nichols*

INTRODUCTION

In that momentous decade between the *Communist Manifesto* and the *Origin of Species,* the Swedish playwright August Strindberg was born. More precisely, it was in 1849, the year of the Gold Rush, of the beginning of Dostoevsky's Siberian exile, and of such a diverse literary market as Thackeray's *Pendennis,* Proudhon's *Confessions d'un révolutionnaire,* and Kierkegaard's *Sickness Unto Death.* It was a year also marked by the death of Edgar Allan Poe, that curious literary phenomenon whose influence was out of all proportion to his essential genius. Alas, Poe died a few months too late for Strindberg to be the reincarnation that, for a few exhilarating months, he fancied himself to be.

Strindberg died in 1912, the year in which China became a republic, Woodrow Wilson was elected President of the United States, and Marcel Duchamps painted "Nude Descending a Staircase." At just that time relativity and psychoanalysis were well on the way to an international reputation, and though Strindberg was, so far as we know, unaware of either movement, he was related to them in a curiously anticipatory way.

During that half-century Strindberg established a reputation for being one of the great eccentrics. While there is a renascence of interest in Strindberg the "psychopath," the fact is that he was very much a man of his time as well as a man in advance of his time. The labile, self-conscious identity of Strindberg takes on special values, if it is viewed in terms of the shifting panorama of the era. In a purely literary way, he reflects a sequence of movements, from naturalism to impressionism to symbolism to expressionism, though not in precisely that order nor in sharp delineation. But he can otherwise be viewed as a kind of cultural landmark.

Strindberg was, in fact, a battlefield of Hegelian opposites. Georg Brandes pointed out that in his face the brow of an Olympian aristocrat was curiously mismatched with the chin of a street gamin; in short a physiognomy where class struggle was plainly writ, a class struggle translated into book after book. On an ideological plane, sometimes Nietzsche is pitted against Rousseau, sometimes Swedenborg against Kierkegaard. However, most of Strindberg's antinomies tend to concentrate in the relationship of the sexes. Strindberg believed in the sweetness of domesticity, but he married one professional woman after another. The conflict between the spiritual and the physical wars eternally in Strindberg and from it springs the passionate love-hate dualisms that made his life a torment, or that he dramatized into a torment.

Quite apart from literature, Strindberg is an interesting chapter in the history of personality. He is a turning point, a watershed between the 19th century past and the 20th century present. Strindberg was one of the last of the polymaths, the Renaissance men who took all knowledge as their domain. Perhaps the very last. Like Goethe, for whom he had a decided elective affinity, he was active in many fields rising to heights of Faustian alchemy and spiritualism. But he could work on more mundane levels. For a time he edited an insurance house journal. As a librarian at the Royal Library in Stockholm for some years, he was ahead of his time. His photographs of crystals and the heavenly bodies are impressive, as a recent monograph makes clear. His knowledge of music was substantial, not so much for the evenings of guitar with Gauguin or the smoky grog-infused nights with that society of friends known as the "Beethoven boys" and numbering some of the best composers of Sweden; but in an assimilation of theory that made him identify the acts of *Hamlet* by Italianate musical terms, compose "chance" music for *Simoon* on "prepared" guitar, and devote his later years to fugal sonatas and chamber plays.

Strindberg was extensively preoccupied with the nervous systems of plants, the manufacture of iodine (in which, he claims, he had a German magnate interested), and the transmutation of base elements into gold. His ideas were hopelessly confused and, though he was able to wheedle laboratory space from the Sorbonne for a time, the distinguished scientist Thé Svedberg has been able to make no real sense out of Strindberg's theories. Nevertheless, the creative curiosity was there.

Strindberg was a Sinologist of sorts, an amateur linguist, a student of symbolic signs throughout the universe ("correspondences," in more than a Baudelairean sense), and ultimately interested in the larger syntheses of world history. Increasingly he used mysticism to reinforce the unseen cohesion of such a system. His mind ranged constantly from the greatest precision and triviality of detail to massive generalizations about the order of the universe.

Opposed to the whole, expansive personality of Strindberg, however, was the fragmentary self, the "characterless character" in his plays and the incomplete man in the world of reality. He was constantly interested in interpersonal relationships, the ebb and flow of psychic substance from one individual to another. His peculiar obsession was, of course, the innate bent of woman to fill her void with all the riches of man. On a personal level it was the vampire complex, on a political level it was the movement toward matriarchy. Nevertheless what is important is the consciousness of a "loss of self," the notion that modern man is the accidental convergence of many forces and drives creating a patchwork character.

Essentially, Strindberg is pivotal between romantic man and existential man. He is still aware of infinite possibility but he is equally and increasingly aware of negative probability, or the great ocean of nothingness that surrounds the island of man. He peoples that nothingness with invisible spirits, both malignant and benign, so it would be a mistake to invent a wholly existentialist reading of Strindberg. These two sides of Strindberg cannot be dissociated; indeed, the partial self always sought to complete itself by identifications with many figures, literary, mythic, and historical. To talk about the anguished Strindberg alone is to ignore the robustness of his character and the healthy diversity of his mind.

Outside of Scandinavia, Strindberg is almost exclusively the playwright. While it is all very well and proper to view him, with Ibsen and Chekhov, as one of the progenitors of the modern drama, his importance as a writer of fiction must be kept in mind. In all, Strindberg wrote approximately one dozen novels and more than one hundred and fifty short stories. How many well-known writers of fiction can claim as much? It is true that half the novels are of such autobiographical character that it is difficult to evaluate them according to the usual standards of aesthetic measurement applied to fiction. It is also true that his short stories range from case history to fairy tale in a manner disconcerting to tastes turned sophisticated by the intricate finger exercises of modern practitioners. Nevertheless we are dealing with a body of fiction that demands its due and is, in fact, beginning to get the kind of scholarly attention it requires.

Strindberg first came to public notice with the satiric *roman à clef The Red Room* (1879), an exposé of bureaucracy and bohemia. It occupies its own significant place in the Strindberg canon, but in terms of influence it is an interesting carrier of technique from Dickens to Kafka, an intermediary in a network of interaction. Among the literature of Strindberg notoriety, mention should be made of those stories which attracted moral indignation, namely *Married* (1884-86). Here it is as if a curious cross-fertilization between Zola and Hans Christian Andersen had taken place to create these acrimonious tales of domestic disaster. *In the Skerries* is essentially a tragedy built around the decline and fall of a Nietzschean exponent of reason. The various novels more specifically autobiographical range from the *bildungsroman* of *The Son of a Servant* to what Strindberg designated as "prose poem" in *Inferno* and that moving exercise in nocturnal melancholy titled *Alone,* its effect much like that of Rousseau's *Rêveries du promeneur solitaire.* Then there is the Gothic detective tale *Tschandala,* in which an ignoble episode in Strindberg's Danish stay is distanced by thrusting it into the 17th century, and the somewhat less Gothic *Gothic Rooms,* a return to the materials of *The Red Room.* The breadth of Strindberg's fiction—as well as the dissidence of its elements—may be seen in one of his best and bitterest novels, *Black Banners,* which is partly a savage treatment of the journalist demi-monde and partly a study of a utopian monastery of the intellect bordering on fantasy. Here, as is so often the case in Strindberg, the world and the spirit war with each other. In his last novel, *The Scapegoat* (1906), Strindberg consciously executed what he conceived to be the Balzacian formula, namely "little people, large ideas." However, his dramatic instincts led him away from Balzac's social amplitude to a circumscribed narrative of tragic dimension. Thus, while

Strindberg was never a formalist in any sense, one can talk about both experiment and variety in his fiction.

The Natives of Hemsö is among the most detached and best organized of Strindberg's ventures into fiction. There is little of Strindberg's own life, at least in the personal nagging details of the moment; indeed there is nothing so intrusive that it demands commentary or draws attention away from the strength of the story itself. The story represents the early Strindberg and is well separated from the upheaval of the Inferno Period (1894-97) .

Strindberg wrote *The Natives of Hemsö*, perhaps the brightest and gayest of his works, during a dark period of his life. He wrote it in August and September 1887 at a time when the deterioration of his first marriage to Siri von Essen was complete, existence was *une terreur,* and there was "death in his heart." The Strindbergs were living in Lindau, Bavaria, at the time, and he longed to escape to the Stockholm archipelago where he had spent so many summers of release. It was a landscape that matched his temperament, a juxtaposition of "the brooding and the smiling, the lean and the rich, the domestic and the wild." The archipelago was probably Strindberg's best therapy. He had every intention of fleeing there, away from "papers, politics, and polemics." To friends he outlined his needs which included, in addition to the proper physiognomy of land, "a broad-beamed, well-endowed woman," free of a husband but possessing children, since he could not work, he argued, without the sound of children's voices in his ears. Strindberg never learned. In any case, it was months before he got there, and meanwhile he escaped by way of a fiction that does credit to his encyclopedic memory for detail—the wildlife, the idiom, the people, the change of seasons—and to the recreative powers of his imagination.

Strindberg's own opinion of the novel was not high.

He described it as "an *intermezzo scherzando* between clashes," the major skirmishes being perhaps
not only matrimonial but literary, since the novel
was preceded by *The Father,* that violent modern
paraphrase of the Agamemnon story, and was followed by the acid accusations of *A Fool's Defence,*
Strindberg's highly personal version of the first marriage. His opinion of *The Natives of Hemsö* fluctu-
ated a good deal in fact, as did almost everything in
his life. In its fashion it was a work of art, but then,
to the Danish critic Georg Brandes, he could apolo-
gize that it was "a shoddy book, written for amusement during his free hours." True, the publisher, in
robbing it of some of its choicest folk vulgarity, was
responsible for making it "conventional, nix, null."

It is doubtful that Strindberg had any premonition
of the novel's future. With the possible exception of
Selma Lagerlöf's *Gösta Berling's Saga,* it is the best
known and perhaps the most admired of all Swedish
novels in Sweden today. Its influence has been impressive. That modern chronicler of the Swedish ex-
odus to Minnesota in the 1860's, Vilhelm Moberg,
author of *The Emigrants* and *Unto a Good Land,*
recently remarked of the influence that Strindberg's
novel had upon him in 1913: "It was the first depiction of folklife I encountered that seemed authentic
and genuine. I was consumed with an astonished admiration for the author's realism. Strindberg went
right to the point and called everything by its right
name. I had never encountered such naked boldness
of expression. That was the way to write! No Swedish
novel has remained so absolutely alive to me as *The
Natives of Hemsö.*"

Moberg was quick to admit that his early infatuation gave way to some serious critical reservations.
Hemsö—actually Kymmendö—was clearly portrayed
by an outsider, one astute enough however to con-
fine his narrative to the summer seasons, which he

knew best, hurrying over the winters. A sharp-eyed, sensitive outsider, yet an outsider nonetheless, who betrayed himself by the curiously stylized language of his fiction. However that may be, countless literary visitors and sentimental voyagers over the years have vacationed on Kymmendö to interview the surviving principals, identify the landmarks, reconstruct the narrative in more than the mind's eye, and imbibe literary inspiration from those incursions of bright water into a landscape now benevolent, now full of harsh reminders of a rocky, Viking past. Werner Aspenström and Stig Dagerman, two of Sweden's best modern writers, replenished their resources at this scene of one of Strindberg's early triumphs. It was a triumph indistinguishable from its setting, which survives in large part by virtue of that setting. *The Natives of Hemsö* is imbedded in the rustic, vacationing, island sensibility of the Swedish people. It is escape literature compounded and of high order.

Narrative is subservient to milieu in *The Natives*. A great deal happens, but the action is conventional and at times manipulated in a fashion repugnant to modern taste. Characters are baldly sketched in, with little psychological penetration beneath the surface. Nevertheless the narrative moves at an accelerated pace, with a kind of zest that transcends Strindberg's occasional nervous mannerisms of style. My *"Abbé Constantin,"* he called it, referring to Halévy's folk idyll, yet if there is a model for *The Natives of Hemsö* it is *Uli der Knecht,* a rustic fiction, an *entwicklungsroman* by the priest-turned-novelist Jeremias Gotthelf, whom Strindberg later described as "a divine Swiss ahead of his time." But Strindberg departs liberally and originally from Gotthelf. Carlsson, his comic manipulator and entrepreneur, has little in common with the stolid and unswervingly noble Uli. They both rehabilitate a farm and rationalize its operation according to modern technology, but that is about all they have in common. It is just as well. Who reads Gotthelf today?

In fact, despite the time of its writing, Strindberg's novel has less in common with Zolaesque realism than it does with the genre paintings of Breughel, as Strindberg himself observed to his friends. Time after time situation comedy asserts itself in fine tableaux. Equally often details accumulate beyond any need of recovery of a *temps perdu,* but to satisfy a powerful pictorial instinct. People matter, and matter in a complex fashion, in Strindberg's plays, but not so much so in the novels.

So far as character is concerned, the novel belongs to Carlsson all the way, and he exercises a measure of fascination. Some have argued—perversely, it seems to me—that he is an incarnation of the incipient superman in Strindberg, on the eve of an infatuation with Nietzsche; but, on the contrary, Carlsson is the egotist-opportunist, adroit drifter, northern picaro who has his momentary successes and then comes to a bad end brought on by a serious lapse of judgment. Carlsson dies, the victim of a *deus ex machina* ending, but Strindberg knew well enough that the Carlssons don't die. They simply move on to another farm or inn, lay siege to another city lass or another gullible countrywoman. It is clear from surviving draft materials that Strindberg at one time intended to resuscitate Carlsson and put his rustic resilience—so unlike anything in Strindberg's own constitution—into a new series of escapades. Interest flagged, and perhaps it is just as well. The play adaptation of *The Natives of Hemsö* suggests that the characters could not survive, divorced from the matrix of a particular fiction and a particular setting close to Strindberg's heart. The novel was a one-time triumph. It could not be repeated.

Ingmar Bergman remarked of Strindberg not so long ago, "There are works of his which can still make my hair stand on end—*The Natives of Hemsö,* for example." He speaks, no doubt, of an aesthetic thrill that is attributable to at least four things: texture of language, power of milieu, comic sensibility, and what E. M. Forster has called "the condition of anonymity." If the first of these is largely inaccessible even in the best of translations, the second is evident, and the latter two will come as a surprise to readers whose image of Strindberg has been conditioned by the plays. For in this novel, Strindberg absents himself with felicity and lets comedy have its way. It is not a comedy of farcical escapades alone, but of man vs. nature. Man the schemer may subjugate, outwit, exploit nature—and his fellow man as well—but ultimately nature wins. The dignity of nature abides.

Richard B. Vowles

University of Wisconsin
Madison, Wisconsin

TRANSLATOR'S FOREWORD

When several years ago I was asked to translate August Strindberg's most popular novel, *Hemsöborna,* I refused emphatically, my feeling being that this brilliant, inimitable prosework of life on an island in the Stockholm archipelago was untranslatable.

The description of the peasant-fisherfolk on Hemsö in the 1880's—then isolated from the mainland in more ways than at present—is easily the most noteworthy and characteristic folk tale ever written in the Swedish language. In it are interwoven comic, farcical, earthy, not to say downright bawdy episodes, as well as painfully agonizing and tragic events, all depicted with such indescribable spontaneity and gusto and incomparable insight into character as to engage and grip the reader completely. Throughout, one senses the author's sympathetic understanding of and feeling for the humble islanders, their seasonal vicissitudes and problems, their joys and sorrows. His masterly depiction of nature in the skerries and its wild life, of sailing, fishing, hunting, farming and harvesting, serves as a background for the story of Carlsson, the ambitious, scheming farmhand from the mainland who for ulterior motives marries the widow Flod and thus becomes lord and master of the farm.

Yet, despite his sympathetic delineation of the peasant-fisherfolk, Strindberg does not gloss over the faults of the natives, their frequently selfish behavior,

and their innate coarseness. As in everything Strindberg wrote, he dissects character and foibles and behavior indiscriminately, without fear or favor, lays
bare their bad traits and praises their good ones; and
the dialogue between the participants in his skerry
drama is flavored with the earthiness typical of people
living close to the soil, always at the mercy of the
elements, and unacquainted with the fancy speech and
polite customs of the drawing room.

Written while Strindberg was living in Lindau, Bavaria, in 1887, this novel was published by Bonnier's
the same year and has, since then, been reprinted in
innumerable editions, including a school edition. It
has also been translated into many languages; as recently as 1962 a new French translation was brought
out. At the instigation of the distinguished actor
August Lindberg—who created a number of leading
Ibsen and Strindberg roles—Strindberg dramatized
Hemsöborna, and it was produced and acted by Lindberg with great success. It has also been filmed in
Sweden.

When I was finally persuaded to prepare the translation, my first task was to prepare a vocabulary of the
many specialized words and terms used by Strindberg:
words indigenous to the locality, as well as botanical,
ornithological, entomological, piscatory, agricultural,
and sailing, fishing and hunting terms. Many words
and terms used by Strindberg not only in this novel
but in other works of his, are today obsolete and not
to be found in any of the modern Swedish dictionaries.
Furthermore, a few of the specialized terms Strindberg
employs are either misused or have been misspelled in
the published text. It is known that Strindberg frequently did not proofread his printed works. Once he
had finished a manuscript, he generally put it aside
and forgot about it, devoting himself to the writing
of a fresh work.

In the decades during which I have devoted myself

to the translating of works by Scandinavian authors, I have learned that—in order to do utmost service to their writings—one cannot translate literally. Yet one must not deviate from the intentions, the poetry, or the rhythm inherent in the author's work. The so-called streamlined translations of great masterpieces of literature current on the market today are annihilations of the very virtues of these works, which have established them as classics. By tampering with the qualities that have made them renowned, translators, lacking in feelings of responsibility toward the author, have often done great disservice to him.

In transposing a literary work of art into another language, there are—as my friend Dudley Nichols noted in a letter to me shortly before his untimely death—"no great translations, only great recreations." What I have tried to accomplish in rendering Strindberg's immortal account of the internal strife among the Hemsö people, their struggle for survival against the elements and other influences, from within and without, is to retell the story as nearly as possible in Strindberg's style and manner. To do so completely adequately would be, as I have mentioned before, an insurmountable task.

For their aid with the translation of the sailing terms in *The Natives of Hemsö* I am deeply indebted to Sven Hansen of the Clipper Line, Robert B. Allen and Gösta Rydin.

A.P.

THE NATIVES
OF HEMSÖ

Chapter

1

CARLSSON ARRIVES
TO TAKE OVER THE FARM CHORES
FOR MRS. FLOD,
AND TURNS OUT TO BE A WINDBAG.

He came one evening in April—came like a whirl-wind, an earthenware jug dangling from a belly-strap slung round his neck. Clara and Lotten had gone to meet him at the pier over at Dalarö in the little fishing dory, but it took an eternity before they were finally seated in the boat. First they had to go to the village store to get a barrel of tar and to the apothecary to get some gray ointment for the pig; and then they had to go to the post office to buy a stamp and to Fia Lövström's down at the bend of the road to borrow her rooster in return for seven pounds of twine that she was to use for fishing-nets—and in the end they had landed at the inn, and there Carlsson had treated the girls to coffee and cakes. And now—at long last—they were in the boat, and Carlsson was determined to do the steering. But as he had never before in his life been in a boat with a square sail, he didn't have much luck with the rudder, and he began shouting orders to the girls to hoist the foresail—and the boat didn't have one, of course.

On the jetty at the customs station, pilots and attendants stood grinning at his maneuvering as the dory sailed close to the wind and scudded before the sea down toward Saltsäcken.

"Hey, there! Your skiff has a hole in her bottom," yelled a pilot apprentice through the wind. "Plug it up, plug it up!"—and while Carlsson was trying to find the hole, Clara pushed him aside and managed to bring the boat up into the wind again; and they glided down in the direction of Aspösund at fairly good speed.

Carlsson was a short, square-framed man from the province of Värmland. He had blue eyes, and his nose was crooked as a door hook. He was gay and full of vigor, and inquisitive, but didn't know the first thing about this sea business. But then he hadn't come to Hemsö to have anything to do with that. He had come to look after the fields and the cattle; and this was because no one there had wanted to bother with the tilling and toiling after old man Flod's departure from this earthly life, and the widow Flod had been left alone on the homestead. But when Carlsson tried to pump the girls about conditions and about this and that at Hemsö, they gave him typical skerry folk answers such as "Well—I wouldn't know about that. . . . Well—I couldn't say. . . . Well—I don't know anything about that. . . ." So that didn't do him much good.

The dory plashed ahead between holms and islets, while the long-tailed duck gurgled behind the rocks and the blackcock crooned among the fir trees in the woods. They sailed across inlets and through narrows until darkness fell and the stars made their entrance in the sky. And then away they went—out into the open sea where the lighthouse of Huvudskär was blinking. They swept past a broom beacon; a little later a white sailing mark, looking like a spook, appeared. One moment they saw the remains of a snowdrift, shining like linen laid out to bleach; in the next, herring buoys rose out of the blackish water and scraped against the keel of the boat as it passed over them. A seagull, startled out of its sleep, flew dazed and frightened from its skerry haunt, rousing mews and sea swallows. The screeching birds made an infernal uproar. And far in the distance, where the stars descended into the sea, could be seen the two eyes of a fair-sized steamer, one red and one green, dragging along with it a long row of round lights, peering through the portholes of the cabins and the saloons.

All these things were new to Carlsson, and he asked about everything he saw. And this time the answers were not long in coming—they came so fast in response to his every question that he could not fail to realize very definitely that he was out of his element, on foreign soil, so to speak. He himself was from the mainland—which to these islanders meant about the same as when a city dweller speaks about someone from the country as a hayseed or a bumpkin.

And now the boat plowed its way leeward into a narrow channel: the sail had to be taken down, and they took to the oars. It was not long before they had reached another small channel; and then they saw a light shining from a little cottage set between alders and pine trees.

"We are home now," said Clara, and the boat nosed into a narrow creek where a passage had been cleared through the reeds, now rustling against the sides, startling a spawning pike which—absorbed in profound speculation—had been circling a fishhook.

A dog started to bark, and a lantern could be seen in motion up near the cottage. The boat was made fast meanwhile at the end of the pier, and the unloading began. The sail was rolled up on the yard, the mast was taken down, and the stays wound about it with belaying pins. The tar barrel was rolled ashore, and jugs, tubs, bundles and baskets soon lay scattered about on the pier.

Carlsson looked around in the approaching twilight and became aware of an entirely new and strange world. Beyond the pier itself lay the fish-well with its winch; and a railing ran the length of the pier on one side. On it were hung cork buoys, ring bolts, grapnel, plummets, sinkers, rope, line, trotline, and fishhooks, while on the pier walk were stacked herring kegs, troughs, creels, pans, and boxes for trotline and tackle. At the head of the pier stood a boatshed, crammed full with decoys: stuffed eider ducks, mergansers, wild ducks, scoters, and garrots to be used in the hunting of sea fowl; and on supports under the eaves lay sails and masts, oars, boathooks, rowlocks, scoops and bailing buckets, icecutters and burbot clubs.

And ashore there was the drying ground where the herring-nets, large as the biggest church window, were hung; flounder-nets with mesh big enough to put an arm through; perch-nets, newly made, and white as the finest knitted sleigh cover; while in a straight line from the pier, like the driveway to a manor house, led a lane, flanked on each side by a row of forked poles on which was stretched the big boat seine. And at the very end of the lane a swinging lantern cast its beams upon the sandy path which sparkled with mussel shells and dried fish fins; and in the big seines glimmered the remains of herring scales like hoarfrost on a spider's web. But the lantern also illuminated the face of an old woman—a face that seemed parched by the wind—and on a pair of small, kindly eyes which had been shrunk and narrowed by the light and the heat of the kitchen stove. And preceding her came the dog, a shaggy mongrel, that was as much at home in the water as on land.

"Well, dear me, so you're home at last," was Mrs. Flod's greeting, "and have you the young man with you?"

"Yes, we are home now, and here's Carlsson, as you see, Auntie," answered Clara.

The old woman wiped her right hand on her apron and held it out to the farmhand.

"Welcome to you, Carlsson, and I hope you will like

it here. Did you bring the coffee and sugar, girls, and
did you put away the sail in the shed? —Good, come
on up, then, and have something to eat." And they all
marched up the hillside, all four and the dog. Carlsson was silent and curious, wondering what the future
held in store for him in his new surroundings.

A fire was burning on the hearth in the living room,
and the white folding table was covered with a clean
cloth. On it stood a bottle of Swedish brandy, corseted
in the middle like an hourglass, and around it were
placed coffeecups of Gustavsberg china, decorated
with roses and forget-me-nots. Freshly baked coffee
buns, and rusks, a butter dish, sugar bowl, and
creamer completed the table setting—which in Carlsson's eyes had an air of grandeur, something he had
not expected to find so far from the mainland with its
solidity and respectability. Even the living room itself
impressed him as he looked it over in the glow of the
sparkling fire on the hearth which suffused and
blended with the light from the tallow candles in the
brass holders and gleamed and glittered in the somewhat dulled luster of the mahogany chiffonier, was
reflected in the lacquered case of the wall clock, sparkled in the silver inlay on the long, damascened barrels of the shotguns and made the gilt lettering on the
backs of homilies, hymnbooks, and farmers' guides
and reference books stand out in bold relief.

"Come and sit down, Carlsson," said the old woman
by way of invitation, and Carlsson, who was of a
younger generation and anything but bashful, did not
run and hide in the barn but stepped forward without
any ado and seated himself on the built-in, cush-
ioned bench, while the girls took charge of the chest
with his belongings and moved it out into the kitchen,
which was situated on the other side of the entrance
hall.

The old woman lifted the coffee kettle off its hook
and dropped a piece of dried fish skin into it, to give a

clear look to the brew. Then she put the kettle back
on the hook over the fire to heat up the coffee and
prodded Carlsson again, this time inviting him to take
a seat at the table.

The new farmhand sat twisting his cap, trying to
figure out which way the wind was blowing, so he
could set his sails accordingly. For it was clear that he
had made up his mind to start off on the right foot
and to make the most of his new situation. But as he
could not know whether the mistress of the farm was
of the sort that would tolerate prattle and small talk,
he did not want to risk opening his mouth too indiscriminately or too soon.

"That's an uncommonly fine chiffonier you have
there," he said as a starter, fingering the brass roses on
it.

"H'm," came from the old woman, "but I ain't got
much to put in it."

"Oh, I'm not so sure about that," Carlsson flattered
her while he poked his little finger into the keyhole of
the lid. "I bet there is plenty of that stuff in there, I
bet."

"Well, maybe there was a farthing or two in it once
upon a time, after the auction was over. But ever since
my man was buried, and with Gusten being away in
the army, doing his conscription service, the place has
been going to rack an' ruin. And then they took to
building the new cottage that was to no use at all—
and so it's been going from bad to worse. . . . Have
some sugar, Carlsson, and pour yourself some coffee."

"You want me to help myself first?" toadied Carlsson.

"Well—since we are just the two of us here," replied the old woman. "Gusten, God bless him, is out
among the skerries with his shotgun; an' every time he
goes hunting, he takes Norman along with him—and
keeps him away from his chores. And that's why
nothin' ever gets done around here. As long as they
only can get out there and take a shot at one of them

birds, they don't care what happens to the farm or the
fishing . . . and this is what I want to tell you, Carlsson: that's what you have come here for—to see that
everything is run right. An' that's why I want you,
Carlsson, to hold yourself just a little bit better than
them, so to speak, and keep an eye on the boys.
—Don't you want to try one of them rusks, Carlsson?"

"Well, Auntie, if that's what you want me to do, to
hold myself a bit aloof, as you say, so that they will
pay attention to what I tell 'em, then it's got to be
done in the right way so that there can be no mistak-
ing about it. And you will have to back me up,
Auntie, for I know these young fellows, once they start
calling you by your first name an' you get to be familiar with 'em." And having said this, Carlsson felt his
feet were again securely on dry land; he sensed he was
beginning to be at home here.

"When it comes to this here sea business, I want
nothing to do with that, for that's somethin' I know
nothing about. But when it comes to the farming an'
I got the ground under my feet—there's where I want
to have my say!"

"Well, we'll settle all that tomorrow when it's Sunday an' we've got the daylight to talk by. Now, fill up
your glass, Carlsson, and then you can go and get your
sleep."

The old woman poured him another cup of coffee,
and Carlsson took the hourglass and spilled out a generous helping of brandy into his coffeecup. When he
had gulped down a mouthful or two, he felt stimu-
lated to resume the broken-off conversation, which
he had found exceptionally agreeable. But the old
woman had got up from her chair and was now fuss-
ing with the fire; the girls were running in and out,
and the dog started to bark outside, diverting the attention in that direction.

"There we have the boys—they're back," said the
old woman Flod.

Voices and the clatter of hobnailed boots against

the rocky ground were now heard outside, and between the balsam plants in the window Carlsson could see in the moonlight the shadowy outlines of two men with packs on their backs and gunbarrels protruding over their shoulders. The dog was now barking in the entrance hall, and immediately afterward the widow Flod opened the door to the living room. In strode the son of the house, dressed in seaboots and a heavy fisherman's jersey. With the proud confidence of the successful huntsman, he tossed his hunting bag and several brace of eider duck upon the table near the door.

"Good evening, Mother, here's some meat for you," he greeted her, paying no attention to the newcomer.

"Good evenin', Gusten. You've been gone a long time," said the mother, returning his greeting, while she involuntarily cast a pleased glance at the splendid drakes, coal-black and chalk-white, with rose-tinted breasts and sea-green necks.

"I see you've had good hunting. Well—here's Carlsson what we've been waiting for."

The son scrutinized Carlsson with small, sharp eyes that were half hidden by pink eyelashes; and his expression, which had previously been open, suddenly changed, and he became timid and distant.

"Good evening, Carlsson," he said laconically and shyly.

"The same to you," answered the farmhand casually, prepared to assert his authority as soon as he had sized up the young man to his satisfaction.

Gusten seated himself at the head of the table, his elbows resting on the windowsill, and let his mother pour him a cup of coffee. He quickly squirted some brandy into it and drank it. All the while he kept surreptitiously looking at Carlsson, who had picked up the birds and was examining them.

"Fine birds, every one of them," said Carlsson,

squeezing their breasts to see if they were well fed and tender. "I can see Gusten is a good shot. He hit them in just the right place."

Gusten accepted this praise with a sly grin, for he could plainly see that the new farmhand didn't know the first thing about bird hunting, when he gave him credit for a shot that had gone in the wrong way and made the birds unfit for decoys.

But Carlsson went on, undaunted and loquacious. He admired the sealskin bags, praised the shotgun, and made himself seem as inferior as he possibly could, as ignorant of the business of the sea as he actually was, and even more so.

"What's happened to Norman?" asked the widow Flod suddenly. She was beginning to be drowsy.

"He's busy putting the things in the shed," replied Gusten. "He'll be here pretty soon."

"And Rundquist's gone to bed—it's about time, too, I should say—and I guess Carlsson could stand a little sleep, too, after all the traveling he's done. If you'll come with me now, Carlsson, I'll show you where you are to sleep."

Carlsson would have liked to have stayed and watched the hourglass run out, but the widow's hints were too plain to be disregarded. The old woman escorted him out into the kitchen, then promptly went back to the living room and the son, whose face now wore his usual frank expression.

"Well, what do you think of him?" asked the mother. "He looks like an honest and decent man, and willing, don't you think?"

"No-o-o, I don't!" drawled Gusten. "I wouldn't trust that fellow, Mother. He's full of drivel—he's a trickster!"

"Oh heavens, what are you saying? Just because he talks a lot don't mean that he can't be a decent man."

"Take my word for it, Mother, he's a windbag,

that's what he is; and before we are rid of him, he'll be giving us a lot o' trouble. But never mind, make him work plenty and hard for his keep. He ain't going to get into my way, that's sure. And you know, you never listen to anything I say. But you'll see—you just wait, an' you'll see. And then maybe you'll be sorry—when it's too late! You remember what I told you about old man Rundquist, don't you? He used the same kind of soft talk. And so we've had to put up with him, and we'll have to go on putting up with him, I guess, for the rest o' his days. That breed of loudmouthed, two-faced scamp is only good for one thing: they eat you out of house and home. And you'll see that I am right!"

"Now, now, Gusten, you talk just like your father. You never believe in the good in people, always expecting what ain't reasonable. Rundquist ain't used to the sea either; he's from the mainland, too. But he can do all kinds of things what the rest of you can't do. And there ain't a chance in the world of getting anyone to help with the sea chores any more—for these days all the sea folk go into the navy and the pilot service and the customs. All we can get nowadays is people from the mainland—and so we have to take what we can get."

"Yes, God knows nobody wants to do menial work no more. Everybody wants to go into government service today—and all the loons and loafers you see out here have come from the mainland. You can't get me to believe that a decent fellow would be coming out here to the skerries if he didn't have some special reason for it—and that's why I say to you again what I said before: keep your eyes open, Mother!"

"Well, Gusten—and you should keep *your* eyes open, that's what you should do, and look after what's yours," the mother harped back. "For it'll all be yours one day, every bit of it; an' you ought to be staying home and not be taking off to sea every blessed day—

and not be taking the people away from their work, least of all, the way you do. . . ."

Gusten, who kept plucking at the feathers of one of the eider ducks, answered: "Well, now, Mother, but you know you like to have a roast on the table after having had nothing but salt pork and dried fish all winter long—so let's not talk about that. And whatever you may say, I don't spend my time going around drinking, you know that—and a fellow's got to do something to have some fun. We've got enough to live on, as far as food is concerned, and a few pennies in the bank, too; and the farm ain't going to rack and ruin yet. . . . And if the house should take a notion to burn down—what of it? It's insured!"

"Well, I ain't worrying about the farmhouse going to rack and ruin—but everything else is falling to pieces. The fences need repairing, the ditches need cleaning out, the barn roof is rotting away so the rain drips down on the cattle, not a ford or a pier is in a fit condition, the boats is going to splinters from dryness, the nets have to be mended, and the storeroom is in need of a new roof. Oh, dear me, there is so much that ought to be done and never will be done! But now we'll see if we can't get it done just the same, now that we've got someone here just to look after all them things. We'll see if Carlsson ain't the right man for the job after all!"

"Well, let him have the job, then!" Gusten snapped angrily, running his hand through his close-cropped hair so that it stood up on end like a spiked pate. "Here's Norman now. . . . Come and have a drink, Norman!"

Norman, a short, thickset, towheaded youngster, with a downy, linten-colored mustache and blue eyes, came into the living room and seated himself close to his hunting companion, after first giving the widow Flod a nod of greeting. And no sooner had the two sea heroes taken out their clay pipes from their pockets and filled them with Black Anchor tobacco than they proceeded—as hunters are in the habit of doing—to review their exploits out in the skerries, giving a shot-by-shot description to the accompaniment of coffee and brandy. The birds were examined minutely, the two lads exploring with their fingers the places where their pellets had penetrated, counting them, speculating about undetermined hits, and making fresh plans for future expeditions.

Meanwhile Carlsson had come out into the kitchen to take possession of his sleeping-quarters for the night. The kitchen was built in log-cabin style and looked like a sailing vessel with its keel turned up as though it were floating on its cargo, which consisted of everything imaginable under the sun. Away up high under the sooty roof-truss, fishing-nets and fishing tackle hung from the beams; and underneath were boards and boat planks stowed away to dry. There were also coils of hemp and flax, grapnel, grappling-iron, pieces of forge-iron, clusters of onions, tallow candles, hampers, baskets, and boxes for provisions. On a crossbeam freshly stuffed decoys were laid out in a long row; on another one were thrown some sheepskins, and from still another beam dangled sea boots, knitted jerseys, shirts, underwear, socks, and stockings. Fastened between the beams were bread spits on which—through holes in the center—were threaded round loaves of bread; sticks, from which dried eelskins hung; and poles, laden with trotlines and ledger tackle.

Close by the gable window stood the kitchen dining table of unpainted wood, and along the walls were three convertible beds, made up with moderately clean, coarse sheets.

In one of these beds the widow Flod had assigned a place to Carlsson, and—after she had departed with the lighted candle—the new farmhand was left alone in the twilight. There was little other light in the room, except for the glow from the kitchen stove and a narrow moonbeam that rested upon the floor, patterning it with figures and squares and diamonds from the window post and panels. In the interest of modesty all lights were extinguished at bedtime, because the girls also had their beds in the kitchen; and so Carlsson started to undress in the dusk. He pulled off his jacket and his leather boots and removed his watch from his vestpocket to wind it by the light of the coal fire in the stove. He had just put the key in the keyhole and begun winding the watch with a somewhat inexperienced hand—for the only time the watch was in actual use was on Sundays and on days of festive or solemn occasions—when he heard a deep, croaking voice rising from beneath the bedclothes: "I'll be damned if he hasn't a watch, too!"

Carlsson gave a start, looked down and saw in the dim light of the fire a shaggy head, with a pair of screwed-up eyes, dangling from two hairy arms serving as props.

"And what business is that of yours?" he shot back in order to show that he knew how to give answer.

"It rings more than once to Sunday service, don't it—even if I don't heed the call?" came from the shaggy head, and it continued: "And he sure is a real cockalorum—with saffian round his boot tops!"

"You're damned right I have—an' galoshes too, if you want to know!"

"Galoshes, too, by Christ? Well, in that case, you ought to be able to treat a fellow to a snifter!"

"I can do that, too," Carlsson replied, setting the question at rest; and he went to fetch the earthenware jug. "Here you are! Help yourself!" And with that he pulled the cork and took a swallow himself, and then handed it to the shaggy head.

"Well, may God bless you, I believe it's nothing less than the real stuff! Here's to your health! An' welcome to the homestead! I'm going to call you by your

Christian name, and you can call me Crazy Rundquist —for that's what they all call me round here!"

Having said this, he crawled down and disappeared underneath the bedclothes. Carlsson finished his undressing and crept into bed, after having first pinned his watch onto a bag of salt and placed his boots plumb in the middle of the floor so that the red goat-skin lining would be plainly visible.

It was now quiet in the kitchen, and the only sound heard was that of Rundquist snoring over by the kitchen stove. Carlsson lay awake. He was pondering the future. What the widow Flod had said to him about holding himself a bit above the rest of the folks and about putting the farm back on its feet again had stuck in his head like a spike. He felt an aching and swelling and festering around this spike. It was as though a growth had taken root in his brain. He lay thinking about the mahogany chiffonier and about the son's whitish hair and his suspicious glances. He saw himself going about with a big bunch of keys on a steel ring, jingling them in his pants pocket; and in his mind's eye he could see one of the hands coming to him for a loan or an advance of money—and then he would lift the flap of his leather apron, shake his right leg, thrust his hand into his pocket and finger the keys close to his thigh—and then he would thumb the keys as though he were picking oakum—and when he had found the smallest one, the one that opened the lid to the money drawer in the chiffonier, he would fit it into the keyhole, the way he had poked his little finger into it earlier in the evening. But the keyhole—which before had looked like the pupil of an eye—now took on a different appearance: it grew rounder and larger, and black like the muzzle of a shotgun—and at the other end of the barrel he saw the son with his ruddfish eye stealthily taking deliberate aim at him, as though to defend his earthly possessions.

At that moment someone came into the kitchen and

Carlsson was awakened from his daydreams. In the middle of the floor, where the moonbeams had now shifted their configurations, Carlsson saw two white bodies standing upright. A second later they dove into a bed, which received them with a loud, creaking sound much like that of a boat sideswiping a shaky pier. After that there were a few lively signs of life beneath the sheets and some subdued tittering—and then at last there was quiet in the kitchen.

"Goodnight, my little doves," came from Rundquist, whose voice now crackled as if he were about to give up the ghost for the night.

"And don't forget to dream about me, like good girls!"

"Ha! As if we had nothing better to dream about!" snapped Lotten.

"Sh! Don't talk to that nasty old fool!" advised Clara.

"You are both so—so friendly and goodnatured! I only wish I could be half as goodnatured as you," Rundquist prattled on with a sigh. "Yes, yes—God knows, when age begins to creep up on us, we don't get the things we like to get no more—and from then on life ain't worth livin'. . . . Well, goodnight now, children. . . . But look out for Carlsson—for he's got both watch and saffian boots. . . . Yes—Carlsson is a lucky fellow, he is! Well, fortune comes and fortune goes—lucky girl who has her beaux. . . . What are you titterin' about over there? . . . Say, Carlsson—how about another swig o' that there stuff? It's so terribly cold over in this corner—there's a draft from the stove!"

"No, sir, you ain't goin' to get another drop, for I mean to sleep!" snapped Carlsson, who had been interrupted in his dreams about the future, in which there was no room for either liquor or women, and where he had already settled himself in his superior position of being a peg above the common herd.

Again there came silence; and only the muffled sound of the two hunters' fish stories about their hunting exploits obtruded upon them through the closed doors of the nearby living room. Intermittently there could be heard, too, the low rattling of the chimney damper in the gentle night wind.

Carlsson closed his eyes and, half asleep, he heard Lotten reading glibly in a whispering voice something he at first could not possibly get the hang of; but as he listened to the string of sounds and words that dragged out into one long jabber, he was gradually able to distinguish the words "andleadusnotintotemptation — butdeliverusfromevilforthineisthekingdom — andthepowerandthegloryforeverandeveramen.   Goodnight, Clara! Sleep well!"

And soon after, the girls were snoring away in their bed while Rundquist sawed wood and gave out snorts and grunts in his bed with such resounding force that the windows rattled. Whether there was any conscious intent or playfulness behind this exhibition of dormant physical strength was difficult to say. Carlsson, however, lay dozing, not sure whether he was awake or asleep until he felt someone lift the comforter, and a chubby, sweaty body creep into bed with him.

"It's only me—Norman," he heard an ingratiating voice next to him say; and then it dawned on Carlsson that he was to have the farmhand as his bedfellow.

"Well, well—if it ain't the hunter come home to roost," croaked Rundquist in his rusty bass voice. "I thought it was Calle who was out shootin' tonight, it being Saturday."

"You're a fine one to talk about shooting—you who ain't even got a gun," hissed Norman back at him.

"You mean to say I don't know how to shoot, eh?" sizzled the old man, bent upon having the last word. "I can shoot an old starling with my backside! Yes—and that from between the sheets, too, if you want to know!"

"Did you put out the fire in the stove?" the kindly voice of the widow Flod called through the door leading from the entrance hall.

"Yes—sure!" they all answered in chorus.

"Well, then—goodnight. . . . "

"Goodnight, Auntie. . . ."

This was followed by long-drawn-out sighs, there was puffing and panting, snuffling and snorting, and soon the snoring was in full swing.

But Carlsson was still only half asleep and lay in that state for quite a while, counting the window-panes to make sure his dreams would come true.

Chapter

2

SABBATH REST AND SABBATH CHORES.
THE GOOD SHEPHERD
AND THE WICKED SHEEP.
THE WOODCOCKS THAT GOT
WHAT THEY DESERVED—
AND THE FARMHAND
WHO GOT A ROOM TO HIMSELF.

When Carlsson opened his eyes on Sunday morning and heard the rooster crow, all the beds were empty and the girls were standing in their petticoats near the stove. The sun, bright and dazzling, was streaming into the kitchen.

It didn't take Carlsson long to jump into his pants, and he went out on the hillock to wash himself. Young Norman was there already. Sitting on a herring keg, he was getting his hair cut by the versatile Rundquist who was bedecked in a clean shirt front, large as a daily newspaper; and he was wearing his Sunday boots as well. With an iron caldron which had lost its legs serving as washbasin, Carlsson performed his Sabbath ablution, with the help of a smear of green soap.

In the living-room window Gusten's freckly face could be seen covered with soap lather. He was making horrible faces at a piece of broken mirror that had come to be known as the Sabbath looking glass, and was slashing his razor, which caught the sun's reflections, back and forth, up and down.

"Are you going to church today?" asked Carlsson by way of a Sunday greeting.

"No, it ain't often we get to the house of God," replied Rundquist, "for we have two long miles to row each way, and it ain't exactly right to break the Sabbath by doing all that work when it ain't strictly necessary."

Lotten now came out to scrub potatoes, and Clara was on her way to the storehouse to get some salted fish from winter storage, a large vat commonly spoken of as the family graveyard, in which all the small fish that had perished in the nets or in the fish-well and for that reason could not be sold, were salted down helter-skelter without regard for heads or tails, in one big mass, to be used for the current needs of the household. There were pale puffy roach side by side with red-eyed rudd, whitebream, ruff, lumpfish, perch, small frying pike, flounder, tench, burbot, and whitefish—and all had some sort of defect: a torn gill, a missing eye, a gash in the back from a stray hook, a heelprint in the belly, and so forth. She picked out a couple of handfuls, enough for a meal, rinsed off most of the salt, and then dispatched the caboodle into the big iron pot.

While breakfast was being prepared, Carlsson had finished dressing. He took a walk up the hill and made the rounds of the farm to inspect the buildings and facilities.

The cottage itself, which was actually two houses joined together, was situated on a rocky hill at the southern and innermost end of a deep, fairly shallow inlet of the cove, which penetrated so far into the shoreline of the island that one had no view of the open sea and might think oneself by a small inland lake. The rocky hill sloped down into a valley where there were paddocks and pastures, fields and meadows, edged by leafy woods of birch, alder, and oak. The north side of the inlet was sheltered from the chill winds by a mound overgrown with spruce trees. In the southern part of the island grew evergreen and moss, and there were groves of pine and birch, and marshland. Here and there, wedged between these, could be seen a tilled patch of field.

On the hillock, in addition to the cottage, stood the storehouse, and a short distance from that another house. It was a fairly large, cross-timbered wooden structure, with a tiled roof, and painted red. It had been built by old man Flod; he had intended to live there in his old age, after turning over the farm to his son Gusten. It was now standing unused, for his widow didn't want to live there by herself; and to keep the many fireplaces going would have required the burning of too much wood.

Farther away, over toward the paddock, were the barn and the cowshed; and in a grove nearby were the bathhouse and the cellar for cold storage, in the shade of stately oak trees. To the south, at the far end of the meadow, could be seen the roof of a dilapidated smithy.

Down by the shore, at the innermost point of the inlet, close to the pier and the boat basin, stood the shed that sheltered the boats.

While Carlsson failed to see the beauty of the landscape, he was nevertheless agreeably impressed with what the terrain might hold in promise. The abundance of fish in the water; the flat fields; the sloping arable land, well protected from wind and already properly graded; the thick woods, with plenty of timber; the healthy trees, ideal for lumber, in the paddocks—all these things gave promise of lucrative business returns if only a vigorous hand were to take hold of the task and bring the buried treasures out into the light of day.

After having rambled about here and there, he was suddenly interrupted in his meditation by a ringing *ahoy* that emanated from the cottage porch and gave echo round the coves and channels. It was quickly answered with a repetition of the same cry from barn and paddock and smithy.

It was Clara's clarion call to breakfast, and soon the four men were seated around the kitchen table. On it stood freshly boiled potatoes and salted herring, butter, rye bread, and Swedish brandy—the latter a special treat for Sunday. The widow Flod went about urging them to eat heartily; and now and then she would cast a glance in the direction of the stove, where feed was being prepared for the hens and pigs.

Carlsson had taken a seat at one end of the table, Gusten had seated himself on one side of it, while Rundquist faced him on the other side, and Norman sat at the opposite end from Carlsson; thus it was difficult to tell exactly who occupied the place of honor. One might have taken all four of them for presiding chairmen. Carlsson, however, seemed to be the one who was conducting the proceedings, for he accentuated his remarks by authoritatively pounding the table with his fork. His topics were cattle and agriculture; but Gusten did not enter into the discussion, and when he did, he turned the conversation to hunting and fishing, and was duly seconded by Norman. Rundquist acted the part of impartial troublemaker and kept throwing a firebrand of discord into the flames now and then. Whenever the proceedings seemed on the verge of becoming too peaceful, he took to the bellows and fanned the flames when they were about to die down, giving a jab to the right and a stinger to the left. He showed the company plainly what stupid and ignorant morons they were, every last one of them; and that *he* was the only one who had any sense, and therefore had a monopoly on brains in *this* company.

Gusten never spoke directly to Carlsson but always turned to one of the others; and Carlsson could see that there would be no love lost between them. Norman, who was the youngest one of the congregation, always calculated on how to stand in well with the young master of the house, on whom, after all, he found it safer and wiser to lean for support and favors.

"You see, breeding pigs when you ain't got no milk in the cowshed—it just don't make no sense," Carlsson blustered. "And if you don't sow clover when you do the fall seeding—how can you expect to get milk? You see, there's got to be *sorcalation* in farming . . . it's got to sorcalate, as they say, in everything—it's got to go round and round."

"Yes, and the same thing goes for fishing, ain't that right, Norman?" said Gusten, turning to his neighbor. "For, you see, you don't lay the herring-nets until after the last catch of flounder; and there ain't no flounder before the pike's spawned. So you see, it goes from one thing to another, as they say—and where one thing ends, something else takes on. . . . Ain't I right, Norman?"

As usual, Norman seconded the motion wholeheartedly, and when he saw that Carlsson was getting ready to plow in, he took up the refrain again, just to be on the safe side: "Sure, there ain't no mistakin' about that! Where one thing takes on, somethin' else lets out . . ."

"Who lets out what, and what end are you talking about?" interpolated Rundquist, who thought it was about time for him to say something. Carlsson, on the other hand, struggling with a fishtail between his jaws and waving and gesticulating with his arms in an attempt to recapture the conversation and row it back to his corner again, was forced against his will to join the rest in the raucous merriment—which was evoked more by spiteful and malicious joy at the temporary burial of the farming business than by the barefaced joke. Encouraged by his victorious sally, Rundquist began to expand and embroider upon the subject he had so felicitously hit upon and from that point on no serious conversation had the slightest chance of finding an audience.

When breakfast was over, the widow Flod came into the kitchen and asked Carlsson and Gusten to come with her out to the barn and the fields to look things over and to see what could be done to put the farm back on its feet, as well as to plan with her how to distribute the various tasks. That being done, they and the rest of the people on the farm were to assemble in the living room to read from the scriptures.

Rundquist lay down on the sofa close by the fireplace and lighted his pipe, and Norman went out on the porch, taking his accordion with him. The others set off for the barn. It gave Carlsson a certain satisfaction to find the conditions there far surpassed his most pessimistic expectations. Twelve cows lay on their haunches, chewing moss and straw, for there was no hay or any other fodder left. Every attempt to get them up on their feet turned out to be of no avail; and after he and Gusten had vainly tried to make them stand up by pushing a plank under their bellies, they had to leave them to their fate for the time being. Carlsson shook his head significantly—like a doctor taking leave of a dying man—but suspended judgment and giving advice until later. The pigs were as lean as hunting dogs, the chickens and hens were running around in the cowshed, and manure was scattered in heaps all over the place, while the refuse water had to find an outlet wherever it could, flowing into puddles and runnels.

Things were still worse with the two oxen, for they had just finished the ordeal of the spring plowing; and the sheep were left to gnaw at the bark of branches, having fed on the foliage until that was gone.

When the inspection tour was over and the premises had been found wanting in every way, Carlsson pronounced there was nothing to do but to apply the knife.

"Six cows giving milk is better than twelve what is starving to death," was his verdict.

With that he started a sightseeing tour of their rumps and udders, and with unfailing cocksureness he picked out the chosen half-dozen—the six that were to be fattened up, doomed to die at the slaughterhouse. Gusten objected strenuously and vociferously, but Carlsson was adamant, emphatically insisting that they should meet their Maker, no matter what. They were to die, as sure as he lived! And from this moment on, there was to be a different order here on the farm! The first thing he would do would be to buy fresh, dry hay before it was time to put the cattle out to graze in the woods. When Gusten heard Carlsson talk about buying hay, he remonstrated to the utmost against paying out money for something they could grow themselves. But his mother told him he didn't understand such matters and bade him keep silent. And after they had made some minor preliminary dispositions for the future, they abandoned the cowshed and marched off toward the fields.

Here long stretches of plowland lay fallow.

"Oh my, oh my," Carlsson burst out with pity in his voice when he saw the primitive methods applied to the good soil. "Oh my, oh my, how childish! No human being lets good soil lie fallow any more—you use it for clover pasture! If you can have a crop every year—why should you be satisfied with having only one every two years?" Gusten gave voice to his opinion that harvesting year in and year out tended to impoverish the soil. Soil needed rest—just like human beings . . . and here Carlsson gave a correct, though somewhat foggy, description of how the clover crops helped feed the soil instead of impoverishing it; and furthermore, how it kept the fields free of weeds.

"Why, that's all new to me—crops feeding the soil,"

spoke up Gusten who couldn't understand Carlsson's learned expostulation of how the various species of the grass family obtained most of their nourishment "from the air."

Next the ditches were inspected, and they were found to be filled with subsoil water, plugged up with weeds, and in need of drainage. The grain grew in patches, as if the seeds had been tossed out in batches, by the handful, and the weeds flourished unmolested between miniature mounds and tufts of grass. The meadows had never been cleared of rocks and tree stumps, and last year's leaves were choking the life out of the grass, which was completely covered by them— all caked together in one sticky mass. The fences were ready to fall down, fords and footbridges were lacking or had disappeared, everything was about to crumble into ruin and destruction, as the old woman had fore-warned Gusten the night before. But Gusten paid no attention to Carlsson's minute and critical observa-tions. He shrugged them off as something unpleasant that was being dug up from the past; also, he did not look forward to the vast amount of labor that loomed ahead—and, above everything, the considerable ex-penditure of money his mother would have to pay out.

A little later, when they turned off toward the cow paddock, Gusten took it into his head to lag behind; and by the time his mother and Carlsson had reached the wood he was nowhere in sight. The old woman shouted a couple of *ahoys* after him, but no answer came back.

"Well, let him go if he wants to," said the widow Flod. "You see, Gusten has always been like that—he's always been kind of easygoing and moody, exceptin' when he can take his shooting-piece and go out to sea, hunting. But you don't want to pay no attention to him for that, Carlsson, for he don't mean nothing by it—he ain't a bad young fellow. You see, Carlsson, it was this way: his father wanted him to be something a little bit better than workin' on a farm—so he just let him do what he wanted. An' when he was twelve, he got his own sailboat, and his own shotgun, too, of course. And from that day on, you just couldn't do a thing with him. . . . But now that the fishing ain't what it used to be, I have to think what to do about the farm—for when it comes to that, the land is safer than the sea. . . . And I think everything would have turned out right, if only Gusten had knowed how to keep after the hands on the farm. . . . But you see, he's too friendly and too easy with the boys—and when you are that way, you just don't get no work done—you get nothing done!"

"No—you can't pamper and coddle them what works for you," said Carlsson unhesitatingly, hooking on to what was in her mind, "and I just want to tell you, Auntie—just between you and me—that as long as *I* am supposed to be sort of in charge here and be bossing things for you, I think it would be better if I had my meals in the living room and slept by myself up in the attic. For that's the only way to get proper respect, and to get things done!"

"Well, now, Carlsson—so far's eating in the living room," said the widow with some trepidation while in midair, trying to climb a fence, "I'm afraid that would never do. The people you get to work for you these days won't stand for your eating separate—you have to eat with them in the kitchen, that's all. Even Flod himself, when he was alive, didn't dare to eat any place but the kitchen toward the end, just before he died; and Gusten has never had the guts to do it. And if you or anybody else was to try it, they'd be sure to kick up a row and start complaining about the food, and you'd never hear the end of it. Yes—so that's out of the question, that's sure. . . . But sleeping in the attic—that's something else, and I'll see about that. Yes—I guess maybe the folks think there's too many o' them sleeping in the kitchen already. And

Norman will like it better, I guess, sleeping alone, with nobody sharing the bed with him."

Carlsson decided to be satisfied with what he had already gained; and so he wisely pocketed the rest of his ambitions for the time being.

They had now come into the spruce wood, where the last remains of a snowdrift, soiled and streaked by dust and pine needles that had fallen from the fir trees, still lingered between two boulders. The spruce trees were already weeping resin in the broiling April sun; and at their feet white wood anemones were in bloom. Under the hazel trees blue anemones peeped out through the webs of broken veins of moldering leaves, while a humid warmth rose from the golden maidenhair. Between the tree trunks a light haze from the fields flickered over the fence leading to the meadow, and some distance away one could see the cove, tinged with blue under the gentle breeze; the squirrels sat nibbling up among the branches, and the green woodpecker kept hammering away to the obbligato of his own shrieks.

The mistress of the farm tripped ahead on the barren pathway, studded here and there with roots and stumps of trees and pine needles, and Carlsson followed in her wake and watched how the soles of her shoes bent with each supple step she took and then disappeared under the hem of her skirt. And it suddenly struck him how much younger she now seemed than yesterday when he first met her.

"You sure are nimble on your feet, and you sure can walk, Auntie," Carlsson remarked in a sudden temptation to air his spring feelings.

"Now, now, Carlsson, you don't mean that. . . . You're just trying to tease an old woman, ain't you?"

"No, no—I always mean what I say," Carlsson assured her in a voice that gave credence to his flattery, "and believe me, if I'm to keep up with you, Auntie, the sweat will be runnin' off o' me."

"Well, we ain't going to go no further, anyhow,"

answered the widow as she stopped for a breathing spell. "Well," she continued, "now you've seen the wood, Carlsson; and there's where we let the cattle graze most of the time in the summer, when they ain't out on one of the islets."

Carlsson cast an experienced eye on the trees and saw at once that they could be the source of many a cord of firewood and that many of them would provide good timber.

"But oy, oy, oy," Carlsson lamented, "you sure have neglected them something awful! And you have twigs, and branches, and sticks of dead, rotten wood lying in heaps all over the place so that neither human being or haycart can get by."

"Yes, you can see for yourself just how things are. And now you can have a free hand and do as you like and whatever you think is needed. I dare say you'll be putting things back in order again, I'm sure of that. Ain't that so, Carlsson?"

"Well—I'll be doing *my* share of the work, if the rest will do theirs. And that's where you, Auntie, will have to help me," Carlsson ruminated, his instinct telling him it would not be a particularly easy job to usurp power and gain his corporalship, in view of the fact that the rank and file were community members of long standing.

Talking incessantly about how Carlsson might be able to hold the reins and maintain his supremacy— an idea which he kept hammering into the old woman as the primary requisite for the impending restoration of the farm—they reached home. And now the day's sermon was to be read; but there was no sign of any of the men. The two hunters had taken to the woods with their shotguns, and it was presumed that Rundquist, true to form, was hiding out on some hillock— for that was his usual place of escape whenever the word of the Lord was to be dispensed. But Carlsson was quick to assure the widow that they could get along by themselves, without any congregation. However, if the girls left the door to the kitchen ajar, they, too, could get a little edification while keeping an eye on the pots and pans simmering on the stove. And when the old woman expressed anxiety over her ability to read the text, Carlsson at once offered to relieve her of that responsibility.

"My, my, my!" he exclaimed; and he boasted that he had read a string of sermons in his day while he was in the service of the public prosecutor in his native province. Thus, as far as the reading of the sermon was concerned, there was no need for any worry on that score. Mrs. Flod brought out the almanac and turned the pages until she found the text for the day, the second Sunday after Easter. She discovered that it was about the story of the Good Shepherd. Carlsson took down Luther's *Book of Homilies* from the bookshelf and seated himself on a chair which he had placed in the middle of the room in order to give himself the feeling of being the center of attraction. He then opened the hymnbook and vociferously commenced the reading of the text, in imitation of the Bible peddlers and evangelists he had heard in the past, and whose technique he had appropriated for himself, his voice going from high to low and running the full length of the scale:

"And it was then that Jesus spake to the Jews: 'I am the good shepherd: the *good* shepherd giveth his life for the sheep. But he that is an hireling, and *not* the shepherd, whose own the sheep are not, seeth the wolf coming, and leaveth the sheep, and fleeth.' "

A peculiar feeling of personal responsibility took possession of the preacher when he spoke the words: "*I* am the good shepherd," and he gazed ominously through the window as though he were reconnoitering the terrain, trying to scent the whereabouts of the two fugitive hirelings, Rundquist and Norman.

Old Mrs. Flod gave a funereal nod of approbation

and picked up the cat and put it in her lap, as though
she were welcoming and giving shelter to the lost
sheep.

Carlsson, however, went on with his preaching, in a
voice quivering with emotion as though he himself
had authored the sermon: " 'But the hireling fleeth' "
. . . "Yes, he fleeth," interpolated the evangelist, em-
broidering upon the text—" 'because he is an hireling,
and careth not for the sheep,' " he shrieked.

" 'But *I* am the good shepherd, and know my
sheep, and am known of mine.' " These latter words
he remembered from his catechism, so he reeled them
off by rote without resorting to the text. Then he put
a sordine on his voice, lowered his eyes sanctimoni-
ously, as though stricken by sorrow over the evils of
mankind.

With unmistakable emphasis, yet with a certain sly,
tacit implication, he glanced to the right and the left
as though he—without exactly wishing to be the
complainant, and despite a pained heart—was making
an accusation against some unnamed rascals.

" 'And *other* sheep I have, which are not of *this*
fold: them also I must bring, and they shall hear my
voice!' " And with a transfigured smile on his face—a
smile of confidence and hope and prophecy—he said
in a whisper:

" 'And there shall be *one* fold, and *one* shepherd.' "

"And *one* shepherd!" echoed the old woman, who
was thinking along lines utterly different from those
preoccupying Carlsson.

With this he grabbed the book of homilies and tried
to calculate how many pages there were to the sermon.
When he discovered it was of an interminable length,
he made a sour face, but he summoned his courage
and embarked upon the task.

The treatment of the subject did not exactly fit in
with his purposes for it emphasized more the symboli-
cal Christian aspects. For this reason it did not evoke

the same lively interest in him that the reading of the original text itself had done, and so he raced through the pages, increasing the tempo when he came to the end of each page. Then he wet his thumb so that he could turn two pages at a time; and the widow Flod didn't notice anything out of the way.

But when he saw that the end was near and he began to suspect that Amen was just around the corner and would come like a bump, he slackened the pace. But it was too late—for the last time, when he thought he had turned only one page, he had turned three. He had moistened his thumb with too generous a helping of saliva, and so he barged into the Amen at the very top of the page, as if he had run headlong into a wall. The widow woke up as a result of the sudden bump and gazed dizzily at the clock, so that Carlsson felt he had better recapitulate the Amen with a few extracurricular trimmings, and so he added "In the name of the Father, and the Son, and the Holy Ghost, for the sake of Christ, our Saviour."

In order to round off the abrupt ending and atone for what he had left out, he read the Lord's Prayer at such a languid, snaillike pace, and so stirringly, that the old woman—who was the target both of the sun and the heat of Carlsson's preaching—dozed off once more, only to come back to life again after the Amen. Carlsson, on the other hand, in order not to have to make any disagreeable or awkward explanations, covered his face with his left hand, filled with an impulse to offer up a silent prayer, which was not to be interrupted by anything of a mundane nature.

The widow Flod—who also felt her guilt—was eager to demonstrate in words of her own choosing what she had gained spiritually. But she was abruptly cut off by Carlsson who—quoting the basic text and the Saviour's own words—demanded unequivocally that nothing more and nothing less would suffice:

there could be only *one* fold and *one* shepherd! *One*
only—*one* for all—*one, one, one!*

At this moment Clara summoned them to dinner
with an *ahoy,* and from the depth of the woods there
immediately came like an echo two identical happy
answers, each accompanied by the firing of a shotgun,
as an exclamation point; and from the chimney of the
smithy, as from a hungry belly, issued forth a grunting
sound—a sound which, judging by its originality,
could have come from no one but Rundquist.

Soon after, the strayed sheep were seen racing to
satisfy their appetites; and they were greeted with a
mild reproach from the old woman for having stayed
away from the spiritual fare served earlier. But they
were all innocent, of course, and protested vehemently
that they had heard no call to come and hear the word
of God—else they would most certainly have come
immediately—without delay.

Carlsson upheld the solemnity of the Sabbath at the
dinner table, but Rundquist prated abstrusely and
strangely about the *re-e-markable* progress in the farming; and Carlsson began to realize that he had been
initiated into and become a member of the opposition
party.

After dinner, which consisted of eider duck boiled
in milk and seasoned with peppercorn, the men went
their various ways, looking for a place where they
could take a nap, and Carlsson took his hymnbook out
of his trunk and then found a spot on the hillock
where there was a dry rock. Seated on this he had his
back turned to the windows of the living room, and
thus he dozed a little while. This exhibition of devo-
tional fervor seemed to the widow Flod a quite
promising beginning on an otherwise wasted Sunday
afternoon.

When Carlsson felt that sufficiently long time had
elapsed to make his absorption in spiritual meditation
seem reasonable and convincing, he rose from his

resting place and entered the living room without knocking. Then, without further ado, he brought up the question of the attic room and asked to see it. The old woman wanted to postpone the matter, giving as an excuse that the room was not in order, that it needed cleaning, et cetera, but Carlsson was stubborn, and finally Mrs. Flod took him up to the attic. And there—away in the back—was actually a tiny, square, timbered box beneath the roof-truss. In the gable was a window, covered by a blue-striped shade. The diminutive room held a bed and a small table; on the latter, placed in front of the window, stood a water decanter. Hanging on the wall was lumped together something which, upon closer inspection, turned out to be clothing. Protected from dust by a white sheet, the collar of a coat could be seen on its hanger while from somewhere else a trouser leg protruded. Helter-skelter a whole stable of shoes, both men's and women's, was placed on the floor, and over by the door stood a huge chest with iron fittings and with a chased copper plate attached to the lock.

Carlsson pulled up the shade and opened the window to let out the foul, stagnant air, which was mixed with odors of dampness, wormwood, pepper, and camphor. Then he put his cap on the table with the blunt statement that here he could sleep in peace; and when the widow expressed the fear that it might be cold up here in the attic and that he might be uncomfortable, he avowed that he was used to sleeping where it was cold, and that he much preferred that to sleeping in a warm kitchen.

The widow Flod thought he was in much too much of a hurry and remonstrated with him that she would first have to remove the clothes so that they would not smell of tobacco; but Carlsson pleaded with her to leave them where they were and promised not to do any smoking. Furthermore, he would not so much as take a peek at them, and under no circumstances was she to go to any trouble and do any moving or make any changes on his account. He would crawl quietly into bed at night, would make his own bed himself in the morning and empty his own slops; and no one but himself would ever set foot in his room, for he understood very well how careful she was about her belongings and that the attic held many valuable things.

When the old woman had been sufficiently bewildered by his incessant prattle, Carlsson went down to the kitchen, carried the chest with his belongings and his jug of brandy up the stairs, hung his heavy jersey on a nail by the window, and placed his sea boots next to the rest of the footwear.

Having accomplished this, he requested an interview at which Gusten was to be present, for the time had come for him to dole out the workload and assign to each man his share of the chores.

After having been hunted in vain for some time, Gusten was finally found, and was persuaded to remain for a while in the living room. But he did not join in the deliberations, and whenever he was asked a question, he answered by raising some objection, or by placing obstacles in the way—in short, he obstinately opposed every recommendation that was made.

Carlsson did all he could to win him over to his side by flattering him. He also tried to break him down by flaunting his own knowledge and experience in farming and by superior airs to instill respect in him for one who was his senior by several years. But it was like water thrown upon fire. It ended by everybody being exhausted, and before they knew what had happened, Gusten had disappeared.

By this time, evening had set in and the sun had gone down, submerged in a mist that before long loomed large over the sky, covering it with faint, feathery clouds. But the atmosphere remained mild and warm. Carlsson strolled aimlessly down toward the fields and came to the ox paddock; then he continued his walk beneath the blossoming, still translucent hazel shrubs which served as a sort of tunnellike roof over the hollow that had been formed in the earth and which led to the seashore, where logs were piled high, to be called for by the purchaser's sailing vessel.

Suddenly he stopped. Between the juniper bushes he caught sight of Gusten and Norman. He saw them standing on top of a rock in an opening in the wood; they were looking around in every direction, their shotguns were cocked, and they seemed to be about to fire.

"Ssh! There he is!" Gusten whispered in a voice loud enough for Carlsson to hear. And Carlsson, thinking it was to him they were alluding, quickly hid himself in the bushes.

But then he saw a bird come flying from above the spruce saplings, slowly and with difficulty, like an owl, its wings drooping; and soon after, another one came flying.

"*Co-norr-orr-orr-veep!*" sounded from up in the air. The next moment there came a *bang-bang* from the shotguns of the two men, and smoke and pellets flew aloft like witches' broomsticks.

A crackling sound was heard from the branches of a birch tree and a woodcock dangled to the ground, only a stone's throw from Carlsson. The two hunters leaped to the spot and picked up their booty, and then exchanged a few remarks concerning their victim.

"He got what he was looking for," uttered Norman as he ruffled up the feathers of the still warm bird.

"I know another bird who should get what *he* is looking for!" muttered Gusten, who—despite the feverish excitement of the hunt—was bitten by other thoughts. "Just imagine—that loafer is goin' to sleep in the attic room now!"

"What's that you say? Is he?" came from Norman,

who promptly scented something ominous in the offing.

"Oh yes! And from now on, there is going to be a new order here on the farm! As if we didn't know better than him what the farm needs! But, of course, new brooms sweep best—so long as they are new! But you just wait—I'll show him—I'll sweep *him* off his feet! I am not going to take a back seat on account of an interferin' busybody like him! Just let him try— and he'll get his fingers burned! —Ssh! There is the other one—he's coming back!"

The two shots had reloaded their guns and now ran back to their hiding-place. Carlsson stealthily wended his way home, determined to take the offensive as soon as he had made the proper preparations.

When he came up to his attic room that evening and had pulled down the shade and lighted the candle, he was, for once, overcome by a feeling of depression because of being alone; and a fear of those from whom he had sundered himself took hold of him. In the past, he had been habitually surrounded by people at all times, had always been accustomed to hearing himself spoken to, and whenever he was in need of a listener he had had no difficulty finding one. Now, however, everything around him was silent, so silent that he, from habit, expected someone to talk to him; and he began to imagine that he heard voices when there were none.

And his brain, which in the past had been able verbally to unburden itself of its thoughts and ideas, now began to fill with a surplus of unused seeds of thought, which kept growing and tried to burst their way out in whatever way they could. And this filled him with such a feeling of discomfort that he could not go to sleep.

He got up and began walking back and forth in his stocking feet between the window and the door of the little room, concentrating all his thoughts on the labors that had to be performed the following day. He planned the various chores in his head, gave out assignments, nipped any objections in the bud, overcame any obstacles—and after toiling an hour, peace and rest were finally restored to his mind, which now felt properly in order again. Thoughts and ideas were categorized and lined up as in a cashbook, in which all the entries had been made in their precise places and added up so that one could see at a glance exactly how accounts stood. This being done, he took to his bed, and when he felt himself quite alone between the clean, freshly laundered sheets, without any fear of being disturbed by anyone during the night, he felt more independent, more in possession of himself, much like an offshoot which has taken root by itself and is about to be severed from the mother bush, to live its own life and struggle through it—with more of an effort, but also with greater zest.

After this he fell asleep, prepared for life's next Monday morning and the toil of the coming week.

Chapter

3

THE FARMHAND PUTS HIS TRUMP CARD ON THE TABLE, BECOMES MASTER OF THE ISLAND PATCH, RULES THE ROOST, AND LEADS THE YOUNG COCKS BY THE NOSE.

The breams were spawning, the juniper trees emitted and divested themselves of their dustlike pollen, the birdcherries stood in bloom, and Carlsson was sowing spring rye where the autumn grain had been blighted by frost. He had dispatched six cows to their eternal rest, and had bought dry hay for the remaining cattle so that they could once again stand on their legs and be let out into the woods. He worked like two men himself and had a faculty for putting speed and energy in people that brooked no resistance.

Born of somewhat obscure parentage on a farm in the province of Värmland, Carlsson showed a decided disinclination and reluctance to perform any menial work, even at an early age. On the other hand, he exhibited a remarkable proclivity for inventing ways and means of avoiding this annoying consequence of the fall in the Garden of Eden.

Driven by a powerful urge to see and learn about every side of human activity, he did not remain long in any one place; and as soon as he had acquired the knowledge he was after, he set out in search of new fields of activity for his ambition and energy. In this way he had turned from a job as blacksmith to that of farmer, had worked as a stablehand, had been a clerk in a general store, a gardener's helper, a railroad laborer, had worked in a brick factory, and finally he had turned to Bible peddling. In the course of all these protean exercises, he had acquired an elasticity of temperament and a capacity for getting along with all sorts of people under every kind of circumstance and condition. He could divine their intentions, read their thoughts, guess their secret predilections and yearnings: in short, these talents of his raised him above the level of those with whom he came in contact. Furthermore, his many varied experiences had made him more capable of assuming the responsibilities of organizing and overseeing things that had to be done; he was not a man to take orders from someone who was his inferior or to be fitted like a wheel under the cart on which he was meant to crack the whip.

Having been catapulted by mere chance into his new position, Carlsson saw from the very first that he might be useful, that he would be capable of turning what was now unproductive and worthless farmland into a source of profit, and that it would not be long before he would be appreciated for this and in the end become indispensable.

In other words, he had now found a definite goal for his efforts and ambitions; and driving him on toward this goal was his certain hope and expectation that a reward was awaiting him in the form of a still better job.

Palpably and undeniably his labors were for the good of the others on the farm, but all the while he kept forging his own fortune. And if appearances seemed to indicate that he expended time and energy in the interest of the widow Flod and her son, this only proved that he was shrewder than many others who might have been tempted to do likewise but who were not clever enough.

The most formidable obstacle to Carlsson's ambitious scheming was the widow's son. With the fisherman's and the huntsman's decided taste for the uncertain, for suspense and the unexpected, Gusten had a positive aversion to anything that was methodically ordered or regulated, or that smacked of security. If you tilled the soil and raised anything on it, you would at best get no more than what you expected, he would argue. Never any more, and most of the time much less. If you hauled a seine or laid a net, you might be unlucky and get no catch, but you might, on another occasion, catch seven times more than you had hoped for. And, if you went hunting sea duck, you might come home with a seal instead; if you lay in wait for mergansers out in the skerries, you might have the luck to bring down a female eider duck. There was always something that turned up, and often something quite different from what you expected. Hunting, moreover, was still looked upon as a pursuit of greater dignity, requiring more vigor and spirit than trudging behind a plow or a manure-cart, for it had been the privileged pastime of the upper classes, from which it had been handed down to the people. This feeling about hunting had by now become so rooted in the people that you sometimes had difficulty inducing a farmhand to drive a pair of oxen —and this may have been due to the fact that the horse, especially the mare, had, from time immemorial, been an object of superstitious worship.

But there was still another stumbling block— Rundquist. Rundquist was actually a sly old trickster who, in his particular way, was trying to establish a new paradise on earth—a paradise where he would be relieved of all odious heavy labor; where he could freely indulge in long and frequent naps, and imbibe alcoholic beverages to his heart's content. By pretending to have a knowledge of occult subjects and by assuming a bantering attitude when it came to anything of a serious nature—especially anything that had to do with drudgery or hard work—and also, if need be, by feigning mental insufficiency and bodily pains and ills—he had learned how to gain his fellow-workers' compassion, especially as this generally took the form of a cup of coffee and a drink of brandy or a generous helping of snuff. Among Rundquist's many accomplishments was his dexterity in castrating both pigs and sheep, and he arrogated to himself the ability to discover water-springs by using a forked twig as a divining-rod and to induce perch to enter a net. He could cure any kind of minor physical ailment but could not get rid of his own. He would prophesy good weather with the appearance of the new moon, after it had been raining for two weeks or more; and when the herring fishing was about to begin, he took up a collection of money from the island folk as an offering to be placed underneath a rock down by the seashore.

But he also averred he had a whole repertory of villainy and wickedness that he could unloose. He could cause his neighbors' fields to be overrun with pennycress, he could make the cows go dry, could cast a spell on people and do other mysterious things. And this helped to make him an object of a certain fear and awe, so that people were eager to have him as their friend. The good points that he possessed and which made him indispensable were twofold: his skill in wielding a sledgehammer in the smithy and in doing carpentry work. But his incredible talent for doing things that showed up most conspicuously, put him in the position of being a rival to Carlsson, and a dangerous one at that; for whatever chores Carlsson performed under the roof of the cattle-barn or out in the fields, they were not the kind that could be easily noticed.

And then there was Norman, a hard worker, who had to be weaned away from Gusten's dominating influence and recaptured for the regular farm chores.

Consequently Carlsson was confronted with a siz-

able job that called for no small degree of statesman-
ship and resourcefulness to ensure success. But as
Carlsson was the most intelligent one among them, he
came out ahead and with flying colors.

He wasted no time on getting into fights with
Gusten; he simply ignored him, after first enticing his
boon campanion Norman away from him through special little favors and privileges. This did not prove to
be a very difficult task, for Gusten was as a matter of
fact rather close-fisted. When he and Norman went
out together on their hunting adventures, Norman
usually had to do the rowing and was never allowed to
fire the first shot. And whenever Gusten offered Norman a swig of brandy, Gusten would secretly take
three himself. For this reason, the advantages that
Carlsson little by little obtained for Norman—a small
increase in wages, a shirt, a pair of socks, and some
other minor things together with the fact that Gusten's influence declined steadily while Carlsson's was
in the ascendence—gradually brought about Norman's defection. When this happened, the son's passion for hunting abated somewhat, for it was no fun to
go out on the water alone. And so, being without a
companion, he joined the others in work.

Getting the best of Rundquist was a task that required subtler and craftier handling, for in him Carlsson had a customer who was both experienced and
cunning. But Rundquist, too, was soon put in his
place.

Instead of offering up money to induce a good
catch, Carlsson had the standnets repaired and the old
warplines replaced by new ones. From then on the
herring was netted in greater quantities than before.
And instead of going about with a forked twig of
parasite mountain-ash in search of new underground
springs, Carlsson had the old well repaired and
cleaned out. Then he built a wall around it and sank
a pipe with a pumping rod to the bottom of the well

and so the divining-rod was thrown on the scrap heap.
Instead of reciting incantations and swinging a flaming stick of wood over the cows' backsides, Carlsson
had them currycombed, and had dry straw put down
for them to lie on. While Rundquist was handy at
forging horseshoes, Carlsson was skilled in making
nails; and while Rundquist was clever at whittling
pegs for the hayrakes, Carlsson knew how to make
both wooden plowshares and clodcrushers. When
Rundquist realized that he had been shunted aside
and when he found himself dislodged from his secret
napping-places, he took refuge in more visible and
showy expedients. He began to tidy up around the
cottage. He cleared away all the litter and rubbish
which the farmfolk out of either laziness or ignorance
had thrown out and allowed to collect on the slope
during the winter months; he busied himself with the
hens and fussed over and petted the cat and put a new
latch on the door.

"Why, just think! What a nice man Rundquist
really is! He's put a new latch on that worn-out old
door," Carlsson heard the girls in the kitchen say.
"Yes, he's not so terrible after all!"

But Carlsson was after him like a hawk. One morning the kitchen fireplace was given a whitewashing, on
another, the water pails were painted green and
embellished with black borders and white hearts, and
on still another morning, the fire logs were piled up
underneath the sheltering roof that Carlsson had
erected on the slope behind the storehouse. Carlsson
had learned from the enemy how to capture the mis-
tresses of the kitchen; and after installing the new
pump-barrel he had become irresistible.

Rundquist, however, was not one to give up easily;
and he was foxy. One Saturday night he had the notion to paint the outhouses a fiery red. But Carlsson,
who had been spying on him, offered Norman a bottle
of brandy, and before dawn on Trinity Sunday the

widow Flod heard somebody moving about outside and a swishing sound against the walls of the farmhouse. But as she was much too sleepy to get up out of bed, it was not until morning that she saw that the outside of the house had been painted a shrieking red; even the window frames and the metal drainpipe were red. And that was the end of Rundquist's magic power, for all time. The struggle had been much too strenuous for a man of his age. He was now laughed at for his singularly precious taste in pursuing his urge for beauty by first prettying up the outhouse; and Norman, like a true defector, made up a joke about him which was retold for many years afterward. It went something like this: " 'You have to start at the right end,' said Rundquist, as he started painting the back side over at the outhouse." —After that, Rundquist lay low, but he was always lurking about, either trying to think up new tricks or figuring out the most favorable way to make peace.

Gusten looked on and let them keep it up. He was satisfied with the way things were going. —"Keep on plowing," he thought to himself. "When the time comes, I'll step in and gather the harvest!"

Up to this time, however, Carlsson's many undertakings had not resulted in any tangible harvest. It was true that the money from the sale of the cows had reposed in the chiffonier for a couple of days and that it had made a very good impression when it was counted up. But it was soon spent; and then, with the widow being deprived of its use, its absence created a void.

But now midsummer was approaching. Carlsson had had many things to take care of and therefore little time for strolling about. One Sunday afternoon he was stretching his legs on the hillock, and as he looked about, his glance suddenly became fixed on the big house, which stood empty and forsaken up there, its shades drawn. Always curious, he walked over to it, tried the door and found that it was not locked. He strode into the vestibule and then came into a kitchen; he took a few more steps and found himself in a large room, which had an air of true elegance about it. There were white curtains, a bed in Empire style, with brass ornaments; and there was a mirror of fine glass, with fancy edges and a carved gilt frame, handsomely embellished—and Carlsson understood that this was something quite grand. Then there was a sofa, a chiffonier, and a tiled stove—and it all reminded him of a manorhouse. On the opposite side of the hall was another room of the same size, with an open fireplace, sofas, a dining-table and a wall-clock. Carlsson's first reaction was one of utter amazement and awe, but this feeling quickly changed to pity and contempt for the owner's lack of intitiative and enterprise, especially after he had discovered that the house also contained two bedrooms with several made-up beds.

"Oy-oy-oy," thought Carlsson audibly, "all these beds—and not a single paying summer guest!"

Intoxicated by the outlook of this beckoning revenue, he hastened to Mrs. Flod and brought home to her the wastefulness of letting the house stand empty instead of renting it out during the summer.

"Dear me, who will want to stay out here?" fretted the old woman.

"How do you know, Auntie? Have you ever tried to advertise?"

"You may as well throw your money in the sea," she retorted.

"You throw nets into the sea, too, if you want to catch something!" Carlsson shot back at her.

"Well, I suppose we could try—but I don't think we'll get anybody!" the widow said finally, having no longer any faith in wishful thinking.

About a week later, a well-dressed gentleman came walking across the meadows, looking about in all directions. As he approached the small farmhouse, the only one to accord him a reception was the mongrel dog, for the island folk—either from habit, shyness, or delicacy—hid themselves in the kitchen and living room, although they had previously been standing in a body outside, gaping at the stranger. Not until the gentleman reached the entrance door, did Carlsson—endowed with greater courage than the rest—come out to greet him.

The stranger had read an advertisement. . . . Oh yes, of course—he had come to the right place! And so he was whisked up to the big house. He seemed quite pleased, and Carlsson promised to put in all sorts of improvements, no matter what they might be, if the gentleman would only make up his mind *immediately,* for there were a number of people who were anxious to rent the house, and it wouldn't be long before the season was over. The stranger appeared to be captivated by the landscape and the beauty of the little island spot and did not delay in coming to an agreement; and after each party had made a few indiscreet inquiries about the other's financial stability and family affairs, he departed.

Carlsson saw him off as far as the gate and then sprinted into the living room, where he flaunted before the widow and her son seven 10-crown government banknotes and a fiver issued by a private bank.

"Oh, but it's a crime to be takin' so much money from people," the old woman whined. Gusten, on the other hand, thought Carlsson had done a good deed; and for once he openly acknowledged his approval when Carlsson recapitulated how he had goaded and hooked the prospective summer guest by inventing a host of speculators who were eager to rent the house.

The money in hand was a trump card for the new farmhand, and after this triumph—which in great

measure was due to his experience as a tradesman—
his voice increasingly took on a tone of cocksureness.
But the cash payment for the rent was not the only
benefit that had been showered upon their little
community; there were many other, indirect advantages to be gained from the rental, and these Carlsson
was quick to point out in dazzling fashion to his audience.

They would now have a market for their fish, their
milk, butter, and eggs; and firewood would by no
means be included in the rent, not to mention any
messages that the new people might want to send to
Dalarö: they would be charged at the rate of one
crown each. In addition, the farm might be able to
dispose of a calf, a sheep, a hen that refused to lay,
potatoes and vegetables. Oy, oy, oy, there was no end
of blessings in the way of profits . . . and the tenant
certainly seemed like a fine and generous gentleman.

On Midsummer Eve the eagerly awaited goldfish
arrived: husband, wife, their sixteen-year-old daugh-
ter, six-year-old son, and two maids. The husband, in
his early forties, was a violinist in the royal orchestra.
He was serene and gentle in disposition, and in easy
circumstances. Being German born, he found it a little
difficult to understand the island folk, wherefore he
restricted himself to answering them with a *schön* to
whatever was said, generously affixing a nod to it.
Owing to this laconic habit, and as a reward for it, he
soon gained the reputation of being a very nice and
amiable man. His better half was a respectable house-
wife who took good care of her home and her children; and with her proper, sedate behavior she knew
how to instill obedience in her servants without having to use tempestuous language or to resort to any
compromising give-and-take.

Carlsson, who was less timid than the others, and
possessed the gift of gab, promptly took the newcomers

in hand, considering this his preferential right and
special domain, since he had been instrumental in
procuring them as tenants, and since none of the others had either the enterprise or the social gifts to be
eligible for the task.

But the arrival of the city folk on the island did not
fail to have an influence upon the habits and thinking
of the natives. To see people in their Sunday best, for
whom every day in the week was the seventh, people
who sauntered aimlessly about, went rowing without
having to go anywhere in particular, who fished, only
to give the fish back to its element, who went swim-
ming, played music, and passed away the time as if
there were nothing to worry about and nothing to do
in all the world, did not at first arouse envy but
merely wonderment that life could be like this. At the
same time, the islanders felt an admiration for people
who had the capacity to shape their existence in such
a way as to live so pleasantly, so tranquilly and effort-
lessly, without ever getting their hands soiled. Especially since one could not point a finger at them and
say that they were able to do so because they had
taken advantage of the poor or done an injustice to
others.

With time, however, the islanders, quietly and
imperceptibly, began to reflect on all this, and they
would cast long, furtive glances up toward the big
house; and if they caught a glimpse of a light, summery dress over by the meadow, they would stop in
their work and stand still, reveling in the sight, as one
does in the presence of something beautiful. When
they saw a white veil on an Italian straw hat, or a red
sash around a slender waist in a boat suddenly appearing between the spruce trees lining the cove, they
would stop their chatter and stand there gazing, with
grave and solemn faces, as if devoutly yearning for
something inexplicable and unfathomable—something to which they felt drawn yet could have no hope
of ever attaining.

The mixture of voices and the din down in the kitchen and in the living room of the small farmhouse now took on a less noisy character. Carlsson began wearing clean shirts all the time, and on weekdays he would appear in a blue broadcloth cap. Little by little he took on the appearance of an overseer; he kept a pencil in his breastpocket (or behind one ear) and not infrequently he could be seen puffing on a mild cigar.

Gusten, on the other hand, kept out of the way as much as possible, for he wanted to escape being a target for comparison. He took a roundabout way in order to avoid the big house on the hill and the light summer dresses, prated bitterly about city folk in general, and—oftener than in times past—he needed to remind himself and others of the money they had in the bank.

Rundquist went about with a dark face and spent most of his time in the smithy, declaring that, as far as he was concerned, everyone in the world could go to hell, no matter who it might be—even the dowager queen herself. And Norman took to wearing his army cap again, hooked a belt round his jacket and made it his business to hang around the well, to which the maids in the big house made trips mornings and evenings.

Clara and Lotten had to endure the snub when they suddenly saw all the males cowardly desert them for the servant girls at the big house, who were addressed as *Miss* on the letters they received. They even wore hats when they went to Dalarö.* The farm girls had to go barefoot, for it was much too muddy and slippery in the cattle-shed and they did not want to risk having their boots ruined all at once. And to trudge through the meadow or work in the kitchen with their feet encased in shoe leather was out of the question; it was much too hot. The farm girls went about in dark

* Instead of kerchiefs, as was customary for servants at that time.—A.P.

dresses and couldn't even wear a shred of white on account of sweat and soot, and the chaff from the hay. Clara had once tried wearing white cuffs, but it was an experience she did not care to repeat. She was exposed in no time and was made the target of grins and sneers because she had had the audacity to show off and try to outdo the others. But on Sundays the two farm girls made up for their drabness by attending church regularly, so regularly that they broke the attendance record for many a year—and all because there they had an opportunity to exhibit their Sunday best.

Carlsson always found occasion to pay visits to the Professor and whenever he passed the house—which was almost continually—he would stop by the enclosed porch, if he saw anyone sitting there, and inquire about everyone's health, predict fine weather, propose excursions, and offer advice and information on the sea fishing. From time to time they then offered him a glass of ale or cognac; but this led to whispered accusations to the effect that he was a parasite, going around angling for favors.

Every Saturday, when the tenants' cook was about to leave for Dalarö to buy victuals for the week, an argument would ensue as to who was to go with her. In the end, Carlsson quite simply decided, once and for all, in his own favor, for the dark-haired little girl with the pale complexion had made a deep impression upon him.

When the widow Flod voiced her objection to Carlsson's absenting himself from his job as overseer for such trivial purposes, he rejoined by saying that the Professor had entrusted him with important letters—a commission he had been asked to perform *personally*.

Gusten, although reluctant, seemed anxious to make the trip and protested that he could just as well be given the task; but Carlsson was not slow in settling the discussion by insisting that under no circumstances would he think of letting Gusten, who, after all, was the master of the house, do chores that could be done by a hired hand; the farm folk would just never stop gossiping about it. And that put an end to the argument.

To be sent as emissary to Dalarö was not without its advantages, as the sly farmhand soon realized. For one thing, there was the sea trip, during which he would be alone with a young maiden and could chat with her freely and undisturbed, and say and do all sorts of foolish things. In addition, it meant an extra drink or two, and a gratuity from the Professor; and at Dalarö he had the opportunity to recommend a new customer to the tradesmen, a favor that inevitably put him in their good graces. He was invariably rewarded by a friendly pressing of the hand, a swig of brandy here and a cigar there; and apart from these material manifestations of their appreciation, the fact that he came as the Professor's emissary and that he shone in fine, handsome Sunday clothes on a weekday, and was in the company of a young miss from Stockholm, surrounded him with an aura of respectability.

The trips to Dalarö, however, came only once a week and they had no other particularly disturbing effect on the daily routine. For whenever Carlsson went to Dalarö, he was shrewd enough to stipulate that the men dig so and so many fathoms of ditches, plow so and so many strips of land, fell so many trees, and when that was done, they would be free from work for the rest of the day. These conditions the men accepted eagerly for then they would be free by suppertime.

On all such occasions, when work was being distributed, Carlsson would inspect it afterward, making frequent use of his pencil and the ever-present notebook. Carlsson soon assumed the role of inspector and gradually transferred his own chores onto the shoulders of others. At the same time he sat himself up more and more comfortably in his attic bedroom, converting it into a regular bachelor quarters. Soon after he had taken possession of the room, he had fumigated it with tobacco smoke and had decorated the table at the window with a small green inkwell, a penholder, a pencil, and a few sheets of writing paper. In addition there was a candlestick and a stand to strike matches on, so that the table took on the appearance of a writing-desk. The window looked out on the big house on the hill; and during rest periods he would sit there, watching every movement the summer guests made, at the same time giving an exhibition of his skill in penmanship—all for the sake of showing off.

In the evenings he would open the window wide and, with his elbows resting on the sill, sit there belching out clouds of smoke from his pipe or puff and blow on a cigar stump he had thriftily saved and pulled out of one of his vest pockets. Sometimes he would take it into his head to peruse a newspaper or periodical; and while in this relaxed attitude he might very well have been taken for the lord and master of the farm property.

But when twilight set in and he had lighted the candle, he would lie down on the bed and smoke. Then he would dream, or rather scheme schemes based on circumstances which had not yet come to pass—but which, nevertheless, might become actuality if he only exerted himself sufficiently.

One evening when he was lying on his back blowing out clouds of Black Anchor smoke in an effort to anesthetize and drive the midges away, his eyes happened to rest on the white sheet which covered the clothes of his mistress's late husband. Suddenly the sheet came loose and fell to the floor. And then he saw the dead man's wardrobe make a flanking movement toward the wall, like a shadowy column of soldiers, and from there turn to the window and back again to the door, keeping time with the flickering of the candle, whose flame was set in motion by the draft. And it was as if he saw the deceased husband in a variety of shapes which the clothes conjured up against the checkered wallpaper.

One moment he appeared in a jacket of coarse blue wool and gray corduroy pants with kneepads, which old man Flod used to wear when he sat at the oars in the boat with the fish-chest and whenever he sailed to town with the catch, or as he sat at the brass rail in Stadsgården, drinking toddy with the fishmonger; the next moment, Carlsson saw him in his black frock-coat with wide, black, flapping trousers—which Flod wore when he went to church for communion and when he attended a wedding, a funeral, or a christening. And there hung the black sheepskin jacket he always wore when he stood on the shore and hauled in the seines in the spring and autumn; there was the grand sealskin coat, vaingloriously sticking out its chest, and still visibly showing the effects of Christmas celebrations, when the final drink for the road—before starting on the way home—was drunk in hot *glögg,* with the outer clothes on; and there he saw the woolen traveling belt,* knitted in red, yellow, and green, coiling and spiraling like a giant sea serpent down toward the floor, its head stuck into the leg of a leather boot.

Carlsson became considerably worked up as he lay there in his shirt, thinking about how he would look in the soft, handsome, silky fur coat. And then there was the sealskin cap—and he thought what a figure he would cut in both, and how he would go sledging across the frozen inlet to visit the neighbors, who would welcome their Christmas guests with lighted torches, set in the snow, and blazing ceremonial fires along the shore, and shotgun salutes. . . . And then—

* A belt used to keep the outer coat from opening and thus letting in the cold air.—A.P.

after he had come inside, into the warm living room—
he would slip out of his sealskin coat and shine in his
black frock-coat and be greeted in a familiar way by
the Pastor who would call him by his first name; and
then he would be shown to the table and be given the
place of honor at one end of it, while the farmhands
huddled together in the doorway or lined up like wall-
flowers on the windowsill.

His visions of these blessings for which he hungered
became so vivid that Carlsson jumped to his feet—
and before he knew it, he had crept into the fur coat.
There he stood on the floor, caressing the cuffs with
his hand; and as he felt the fur collar tickling his
cheek, he gave a ululant squeal of excitement. Then he
wriggled into the black frock-coat and buttoned it,
placed his shaving mirror on the chair, twisted about
to see how the coat fitted in the back, struck a Napo-
leonic pose with his hand inside the lapel, and
strutted back and forth across the floor. The smooth
nap of the cloth imparted a feeling of opulence, a
sensation not only of comfort but of generous proportions which he experienced when he tried to separate
the tails as he sat down on the edge of the bed, imag-
ining that he was paying a formal visit at someone's
house.

As he sat there, deep in intoxicating dreams, he
heard the sound of gay voices outside. All ears, he
recognized Ida's voice—Ida was the pretty little cook
—mingling with that of Norman. Their voices seemed
to join as if in vocal tandem, seemed fused, almost as
if their lips were meeting. It cut him to the quick. In
the twinkling of an eye he had returned the fineries to
their hangers beneath the dust sheet. And armed with
a freshly lit cigar, he went downstairs.

Being forever occupied with momentous projects
and schemes for the future, Carlsson had up to now
steered clear of any and all dealings with the girls. For
he knew how much time could be spilt if one became

involved in such matters. He was also aware of the
fact that the moment he opened fire in that direction,
he would run the risk of exposing himself in some
sensitive spot that he would find hard to defend. Besides, if he should be checkmated playing that game
and suffer a downfall, he would lose their respect, and
his authority over them would be gone. On this occasion, however, when the beauty in question had laid
herself open to a general competition in which the
victor had so much to gain, Carlsson felt compelled to
use his spurs and boldly go to the attack. And mili-
tantly determined to be the top rooster, he wended his
way to the hillock, where the firewood was kept and
where the frolicking was already underway. It pro-
voked him to think that he would be pitting his clev-
erness and wits against a nobody like Norman. Had it
at least been Gusten—but that little squirt Norman
. . . well, he would show him!

"Good evening, Ida!" he began, showing no sign of
noticing his rival, who—against his will—gave up his
perch on the fence, which Carlsson unhesitantly annexed.

And now Carlsson, aided and abetted by his superior talent for conversation, began playing his game;
and all through it, Ida went about her work, heaping
logs and sticks of wood in her basket. And Norman
never had a chance to say a word. But Ida was as
shifty as someone who had been moonstruck and she
kept throwing asides to Norman. Carlsson, however,
seized them in midair and volleyed them back to her
with additional frills and pretty, colorful embellish-
ments. Then the pretty little damsel, who enjoyed their
tug-of-war, asked Norman to splinter some wood to
start the fire with. But before the chosen lucky one
was able to reach the gate, Carlsson had already
climbed over the jagged, rough-hewn fence, pulled out
his clasp-knife, cut off a dry spruce branch, and splin-
tered it. Within a few short minutes, he had filled the

basket; then he lifted it with his little finger and in this way carried it straight into the kitchen, with Ida tripping behind him.

There he took up his stand in the doorway, arching his back and leaning against the post so that no one could either come in or go out. Norman, who could not think up any errand that would gain him admittance, at first aimlessly circled the pile of fire-logs on the hillock, splenetically reflecting upon the ease with which the bold and the brazen succeeded in life. Finally, however, he marched off, went over to the well, sat down on the big tub, and gave vent to his grief by playing a schottische which he blared out on his accordion.

The softly tender tones that emanated from the brass tongues of his instrument floated on the heavy evening air past the sentry guarding the doorway and reached the throne of mercy by the kitchen stove. This was evidenced by the fact that Ida suddenly remembered that she had to fetch the Professor his decanter of fresh drinking water from the well. Carlsson trotted along, this time, however, with somewhat less assurance, for on the battlefield of music he was not at all at home. In order to soften the impact of the alluring sounds from the accordion, he carried Ida's copper decanter, all the while whispering tender words into her ear in the most dulcet and honeyed tones he could muster—as though he were improvising words to the seductive music and trying to relegate Norman's solo to the status of mere accompaniment to his own star performance. But no sooner had they come to the well than they heard the widow Flod calling to them from the farmhouse. It was Carlsson she wanted to see, of course, and from her tone it sounded as though the matter in question was urgent. At first he was annoyed and decided not to answer, but then the devil took hold of Norman and he sang out in stentorian tones:

"He's here, Auntie! He'll be with you in a jiffy!"

Without giving voice to his feelings, the victor consigned the perfidious accordion player to Hades, while silently damning him an unprecedented number of times. He, the victorious one, now had to tear himself from the arms of love and abandon his half-won quarry to a second-rater who had nothing but chance to thank for his luck in love.

The old woman called again, and this time Carlsson answered irritably that he was hurrying as fast as he could. Mrs. Flod received him on the doorstep, shading her eyes with her hand as if to penetrate the fair summer twilight and to make sure that he had come alone.

Ordinarily, Carlsson was only too glad to accept a drink of something strong, but this time he would have liked to dispatch both coffee and liquor to an unmentionable destination. However, he could not say no to her; and so—to the accompaniment of the March of the Norrköping Sharpshooters, played triumphantly and tantalizingly by Norman, rolling down from where he was seated at the well—he was obliged to step inside. The widow was even more affable than usual, but at the same time she appeared older and uglier to him; and the more she tried to please him, the more blunt and obstinate he became, and this had the effect of making the widow almost tender.

Finally she came to the point, while she poured the coffee.

"You see, Carlsson, it's this way: we are inviting people to the haymaking next week, and that is why I want to have a talk with you first, of course."

At this moment the accordion came to a stop in the middle of the mellifluous chords of the trio and Carlsson stiffened, his face became motionless, and his attention was diverted elsewhere. He chewed on his words and finally produced a few flat ones, lacking in resonance and without any strict coherence.

"So-o . . . is that so—yes—yes—the haymaking—oh yes, next week."

"And so I thought," the old woman continued, "that you might take Clara with you this Saturday and go 'round to the neighbors and invite them. And at the same time I thought it would be good for you to get out a little and get to know people 'round here. For, you see, it's always good for you to show yourself a bit, Carlsson. . . ."

"Well, but Saturday is out of the question, for that's the day I'm supposed to go to Dalarö for the Professor and his wife," Carlsson answered.

"Well, don't you think that Norman could take care of that chore, for once?" the widow Flod retorted, quickly turning her back to him in order not to see his sour face.

In the same breath the accordion began wheezing out a few tender, sentimental interludes, interrupted now and then by a pause. The music seemed to be disappearing into the distance, to be fading away in the summery night air, while from afar the nightjar could be heard buzzing and spinning.

Carlsson, sweating like a man in the throes of death, gulped down the coffee and the brandy. He felt as if a heavy stone were on his chest; his mind was muddled and befogged, and he felt weak and nervous and upset.

"Norman couldn't do that!" ejaculated Carlsson. "Norman wouldn't know how to transact all the Professor's errands—and—and besides—the Professor don't think he's dependable . . ."

"Well, but I have talked with the Professor," the old woman interrupted him, "and he said there was nothing he needed from Dalarö this Saturday."

Carlsson was done for. The widow had tricked him into her trap like a mouse, and it was too late for him to find a hole to creep into. Besides, his thoughts and senses were focused on other things than the trip to Dalarö, and he could not collect his wits sufficiently to answer her. He couldn't find words to make a counterattack. The widow Flod noticed this, and promptly took to kneading while the yeast fermented.

"Listen to me, Carlsson," she said, "I don't want you to take offense if I tell you something now . . . for I'm doing it for your own good."

"You can tell me whatever you feel like, Auntie, no matter what," Carlsson burst out as the accordion player's tender love tunes became more intense and gradually faded away toward the far reaches of the paddock.

"Well, all I want to say, Carlsson, is that you ought to hold yourself much too good to be playin' 'round with them girls. For it'll never end well. It'll lead to nothing but grief and trouble. Oh yes, oh yes, I know . . . I know what I'm talkin' about, and I am telling you for your own good, Carlsson. Them girls from the city, they always want to have a long train of menfolk in their wake or they ain't satisfied. And then they want to be fussed an' fidgeted over, and then there'll be a lot of fiddle-faddle goin' on. . . . An' if they slink into the woods with one, they go into the grove or the paddock with another; an' if it leads to somethin' what they don't expect, they put the blame on the one they think is the easiest to hook. Yes, that's the way it always goes. . . ."

"Well, I don't give a damn what the boys do. That's none of my business," Carlsson muttered.

"Now, now, you mustn't get so stirred up," the widow said, trying to mollify him. "The thing is you are the sort of man, Carlsson, what ought to be thinking of getting married; and that's why you shouldn't have nothing to do with wenches and strumpets and females like that. And let me tell you—out here in the skerries you'll find plenty of girls with money. And if you keep your wits about you, Carlsson, and if you know how to make hay while the sun shines, you may get to have your own farm before you know it. And that's the reason you shouldn't be so obstinate but pay attention and listen to me when I tell you I want you to go 'round to the neighbors and invite 'em to the haymaking. And I want to make it plain, I wouldn't ask just anybody to go on an errand like that; and I wouldn't be surprised if Gusten made a fuss about it. But I ain't goin' to pay no attention if he does, for if I once make up my mind about someone, I stick to him, you can depend on that!"

When Carlsson heard this, he calmed down, for he began to sense something of superior advantage and profit to him by acting in such an important capacity for the farm.

But he was still too resentful to think of bartering his burning passion for something so nebulous, and he felt he ought to have some sort of advance payment before he even considered letting himself be dragged into any kind of deal.

"How can I go 'round seeing people the way I look, having no decent clothes?" he said, throwing out his baited fishhook.

"Oh, I don't think your clothes are so bad as all that," the widow offered as her opinion, "but if that's all you're worryin' about, I guess we can fix that somehow."

Carlsson was not tempted to proceed any further in that direction and resolved instead to trade the half-promise the widow had just given him for another one; and after bickering hither and thither he succeeded at last in gaining his point that Norman was to remain at home because of his dexterity in sharpening scythes and in repairing haycarts—jobs for which he was irreplaceable—while Lotten was to be sent to Dalarö to do the errands.

It was three o'clock in the morning on one of the
first days of July. The smoke was already coming out
of the chimney, and the big coffeepots were on the
stove. Everybody in the house was awake and moving
about, and out on the hillock a long table had been
put up and was already set with dishes and coffeecups.
The haymakers, who had arrived the evening before,
had spent the night up in the hayloft and in the barn.
Outside the farmhouse, standing in groups, were
twelve towering islanders in their white shirtsleeves
and straw hats and armed with scythes and whetstones
to sharpen them with. There you could see the neighbors from Åvassa and Svinåker, old before their time
and bent over from rowing; you saw the neighbor
from Aspö with his flowing Viking beard, taller than
the rest by a head, his eyes bearing an introspective
expression which came from his lonely life out there
by the open sea, from sorrows and misfortunes never
given voice; there was the man from Fjällång, angular
and twisted like a dwarfed pine tree far out on the
last rocky islet in the sea, and the native of Fiversätra
Island, who had weathered many a storm out there.
Dried up like the fish-skin the natives put in their
coffee, he was lively despite his skinniness. The men
from Kvarnö, known for their boatbuilding, were
there, too; and the champion seal hunters from Lång-
viksskär; and the farmer from Arnö, with his sons.
Shuttling between them and skipping about were the
girls in their light-colored cotton dresses with white
sleeves, and with kerchiefs crisscrossed over their
bosoms, and large kerchiefs about their heads. Each
girl had brought her own hayrake; these were freshly
painted in all the colors of the rainbow and looked
more as if they were to be used for some festive occasion than for work. The old men poked their knuckles
into the girls' ribs and whispered good-natured jokes
to them, but the boys and the young men kept their
distance, in view of the early morning hour, biding

the time for their lovemaking until evening set in with its twilight, dancing, and music. The sun had been up a quarter of an hour but had not yet reached above the pines on top of the hill so that it could lick the dew from the grass; the cove lay shining like a mirror within its frame of reeds, now turned a pale green, and you could hear the newly hatched duck-lings peeping and cheeping an obbligato to the quack-ing and gabbling of the older generation; the great white gulls came sailing through the air on snowy white wings spread wide like the plaster of Paris angels in church, and swooped down into the water to catch an alburn; the magpies had awakened from their slumber in the oak tree by the cellar and were gossiping and chattering about the many shirtsleeves they had seen down on the slope by the farmhouse; the cuckoo, madly in heat, cuckooed frantically in the paddock as if he wanted to voice his opposition to the end of the mating season, which would come at the sight of the first stack of hay; the corncrake croaked and quaked over in the rye field; and up on the hill the mongrel kept welcoming old acquaintances. And white shirtsleeves and linen-wear gleamed and glis-tened in the sunshine, as arms were stretched across the coffee table, where cups and saucers, glasses and coffeepots clattered and rattled while breakfast was being served. Gusten, who ordinarily was bashful, acted as host for the occasion. Because he felt at home with these men, who were old friends of his father, he willfully disregarded Carlsson and took charge of the brandy bottle himself. But Carlsson, who had already become acquainted with some of them while on his trip to extend the invitations to the haymaking, got on with them as though he were an older relative and let himself be fussed over. Being ten years older than Gusten and having the appearance of a mature man he had no difficulty in relegating Gusten to the back-ground; for to these men, who had been close friends of his father, Gusten could never be anything but a boy.

The coffee had now been downed, the sun was coming up, and the older men, shouldering their scythes, began to move toward the big field, followed by the younger men, the boys, and the girls.

The grass reached all the way up to their thighs and was thick as a pelt, so that Carlsson was urged to give details of his new system of feeding and caring for the meadows: how he had the farmhands clear away leaves and last year's grass, level off the molehills, plant seed in the frosted patches, and water it all down with liquid manure. After that he gave orders to the men, much like a captain gives orders to his company, assigning the place of honor to the oldest and the richest among them, and seeing to it that he got a place at the end of the honor brigade so that he would not be lost in the crowd.

And then the advance began. Two dozen white shirtsleeves went forward like a wedge, like swans migrating in the fall, the scythes heel to heel. In their wake, keeping a distance from one another, and spread out like a flock of terns, came the girls with their rakes, playfully pitching and tossing the hay, yet not scattering it, each girl behind her male partner.

The scythes produced a whistling and whizzing, and the dew-soaked grass fell in heaps. Alongside the hay lay all the blossoms of summer that had ventured outside the paddock and the woods: white daisies and bitter vetch, limewort and Our Lady's bedstraw, wild chervil, vetch and maiden-pink, purpled cow-wheat, tufted vetch, butterbur, clover, and all the sedges and grasses of the fields and meadows. There was a fragrance in the air, sweet as honey and spices: bees and bumblebees fled in swarms before the murderous onslaught; the moles crept down into the entrails of the earth when they heard their fragile roof begin to collapse; the ringed snake darted in fright into the ditch and slithered into a hole like the tail-end of a rope. High above the battlefield a pair of titlarks pivoted about in the air after their nest had been trampled and destroyed by a haymaker's heel; and at the end of the brigade, like a rear guard, closing up the ranks, the starlings came tripping, picking and pecking and nibbling at all sorts of creeping and crawling creatures which now lay in full view, spotlighted by the blazing sun.

The first attack took the haymakers as far as the edge of the field, and now the warriors, leaning on the handles of their scythes and wiping the sweat from the leather sweatbands inside their hats, paused for a brief rest and surveyed the destruction they had wreaked. Then they each took a pinch of snuff from their brass snuffboxes and administered it between their jaws; meantime the girls hastened to catch up with the vanguard.

And then the second attack began across the verdant sea of flowers which in the increasing morning breeze now flowed in ripples, appearing in a multiplicity of colors wherever the hardier stalks and the heads of blossoms protruded through the waves of soft grass, which made way for the breeze and now stretched out in an unchanging surface of green, like a becalmed sea.

There was excitement and a spirit of contest and festivity in the air; there was not a haymaker who would not have preferred being a victim of sunstroke to laying down his scythe.

Carlsson had been given the Professor's Ida as his raking partner; and, being the last in the line, he could—whenever he was tempted to show off—turn around and say a word or two to her, with no danger of his calves being exposed to anyone's scythe. Diagonally ahead of him was Norman, and Carlsson kept a strict watch on him. Whenever Norman was tempted to cast an enamored glance in a southeasterly direction, Carlsson was promply at his heels with a cry of warning, which smacked more of unfriendliness than of good intentions: "Watch out for your heels!"

By eight in the morning the meadow near the spring had the appearance of newly drilled arable land. It was flat as a hand, and the hay lay in long swaths. Now the haymakers looked over their handiwork and examined the workmanship; and Rundquist found himself singled out for incompetence by those chosen as judges. Wherever he had advanced with his scythe, you could see ring after ring of tufts and patches of grass that he had left standing. Rundquist defended himself by saying that he just couldn't take his eyes off the girl who had been assigned to him— after all, it was not every day that he had a girl at his heels.

At this moment, Clara let out an *ahoy,* calling the haymakers to breakfast up on the hill. The brandy bottle glimmered in the sun, and the keg of near-beer was opened; the potatoes steamed in the caldron on the hearthstone, and the herrings clouded the plates with moisture; butter had been placed on the table, the bread had been cut, the brandy had been passed, and the meal was underway.

Carlsson had had praise heaped on him and was intoxicated by his victory. To boot, Ida seemed to be favoring him, and his amorous attentions to her could not but be noticed. But then she was, in fact, the beauty of the day. Old Mrs. Flod kept running in and out with platters and plates and would ever so often pass close to Carlsson and Ida—much too often not to have Ida notice it; but Carlsson was not conscious of this until the old woman jabbed him in the back with her elbow and whispered: "You know, Carlsson, you are to act as host today and give Gusten a helping hand! You have to show you are at home here!"

Carlsson, however, had neither eyes nor ears for anyone but Ida and answered the widow with a jesting remark. Just then the Professor's nursemaid came up and brought a reminder to Ida that she was to go home and look after the house. This perturbed and grieved the men, but the girls showed no particular signs of sorrow.

"Who's going to pick up the hay for me now when my girl is gone?" Carlsson exclaimed, feigning despondency in order to hide his vexation and resentment, which were his real feelings.

"I suppose Auntie will have to do it, I guess," volunteered Rundquist, who was said to have eyes in the back of his head.

"Auntie knows how to rake! Let her do it!" yelled the menfolk in chorus, "Auntie is going to rake!" —The old woman made a disparaging gesture with a shake of her apron.

"God bless me, you want an old woman like me to go raking with the girls! No, no—never in this life— never! Why, you must be out of your mind!"

But they kept goading and teasing her.

"Go ahead and take the old woman!" Rundquist urged in a whisper, while Norman kept encouraging him and Gusten's countenance turned dark as night.

Carlsson had no choice; and to the accompaniment of boisterous laughter and noisy outcries Carlsson sprinted down to the farmhouse to look for the old woman's rake, which was stored away somewhere in the attic. The widow scuttled after him, shrieking:

"For God's sake—no—I won't let you go rummaging through my belongings up there!" And then they both disappeared, followed by the loud and biting remarks of those who stayed behind. During the silence that finally set in, Rundquist suddenly interjected, "It seems to me . . . it seems to me they are staying up there a long time. Go down and see what's happened to them, Norman!"

Vociferous applause egged the old exhibitionist on and he continued:

"What do you suppose they can be doing up there, eh? Why, this'll never do! I'm getting worried, I tell you!"

Gusten's lips turned blue-black, but he forced himself to join in the laughter in order not to stand apart from the rest.

"May the Lord forgive me my sins," Rundquist went on in the same vein, "but I just can't stand not knowing what's goin' on—I just got to go and find out for myself what they're doing!"

At this very moment Carlsson and the widow came out of the house together. Carlsson carried the rake he had gone to look for, and it was a fine one, decorated with two painted hearts and inscribed *Anno 1852*. It had been given to the widow by old man Flod when they were engaged, and he had made it himself. Inside the knob of the handle were dried peas, and whenever anyone touched the rake, the peas rattled. Remembrance of the joys and ecstasies of days now past appeared to have put the old woman, who still possessed a lively disposition and spirit, in a good humor. Without any trace of sickly sentimentality, she pointed to the date on the rake, and said:

"You see—it wasn't yesterday that Flod made this rake . . ."

"And when you climbed into the bridal bed, Auntie," the neighbor from Svinåker interjected.

"And may well climb in again," added the man from Åvassa.

"There are two things you can't rely on: six-week-old pigs and two-year-old widows," teased the farmer from Fjällång.

"The drier the tinder, the easier it sets on fire," chimed in the fisherman from Fiversätra Island.

Each man threw his little twig into the fire, yet the old woman only smiled a beaming smile and refused to be upset, as she joined in the banter, feeling it wasn't anything worth getting angry about. And now they set off for the marshfield where sedge and scouring rush stood like a forest of pine trees. The water reached all the way to the top of the men's boots, so the girls removed their shoes and stockings and hung them on the fence.

The old woman kept raking away and never stopped, so that she was at Carlsson's heels all the time; and this evoked much jesting about the young pair, as they were called.

Midday came and went, and then evening set in. The fiddler arrived with his fiddle, the barn was swept and cleared, and the worst of the knotholes and knags were filled in with pitch; and as soon as the sun had set, the dancing commenced.

Carlsson opened the dancing with Ida, who was wearing a black dress that had a square neck with white ruching and a Mary Stuart collar. The dress made her stand out among the farm girls as if she were some enviable lady, and while the older people looked at her with a mixture of awe and apprehension and treated her with frigidity, the youths eyed her lustfully.

Carlsson was the only one who knew how to dance the latest waltz, and after Ida had unsuccessfully tried an old-fashioned three-step with Norman, she was glad to accept Carlsson's invitation to dance with him again and again. Feeling himself insulted and checkmated, Norman then hit upon the mischievous notion of resorting to his accordion—not only to give musical expression to the pangs of his broken heart, but also to allow the dulcet tones to serve as a lover's lime-twig in a last attempt to catch the fickle, pretty little bird who he had thought not so many weeks ago was already in his hand; but she had flown away and he now saw her sitting on the roof exchanging smacking kisses with another man. In Carlsson's estimation, Norman's accompaniment was totally unnecessary and presumptuous since Carlsson had gone out of his way to hire an expert musician; and the halting, heaving chest tones from the accordion were not, as a matter of fact, exactly in step or in tune with the lightfooted fiddle. The accordion interfered with the swinging rhythm and brought disarray and confusion into the dancing. Scenting a favorable opportunity to put his rival out of commission, especially since the others seemed to share his opinion of the instrumentalist's incompetence, Carlsson's tongue began to swell with words aching to be released, and with a shriek he ejected them across the barn to the miserable lover, who sat huddled in the corner:

"Hey, you—put a lock on that leather bag of yours! And if you are full of wind, go out on the hill and squeeze it out of yourself there!"

This indictment met with heavy response from the company, which grinningly excoriated the sinner. But Norman had had a few drinks, and Ida's square-necked dress had magically summoned forth in him an unsuspected store of inner strength; consequently he was not inclined to bite the dust at Carlsson's challenge.

"Hey, you!" he shot back in a mimicking tone to Carlsson, who had unconsciously reverted to his native speech—a dialect that was always ridiculed by people who came from other provinces than Carlsson's Värmland.

"Come out on the hillside, and I'll take the fleas out of your hide, you swine!"

Carlsson did not judge the situation dangerous enough to require the use of fists and so he stayed within the more innocent range of verbal sparring, engaging only in vituperative epithets.

"It must be a peculiar sort of pig what has its hide full of fleas. Where do them pigs come from?" Carlsson queried.

"I can tell you that easy enough—from Värmland!" Norman shot back. This remark pricked Carlsson's native pride and honor, and still searching vainly for a withering rejoinder that would deal a deathblow to his adversary, he advanced straight toward the enemy, took hold of him by the vest, and dragged him out of the barn in the direction of the hillside.

The girls gathered in the doorway to get a good view of the fight, and no one showed the slightest inclination to try to stop it.

Norman was short and squat, but Carlsson was more mature and more powerfully built. In the twinkling of an eye he took off his jacket, not wanting to get it mussed or soiled, and the two flew at each other— Norman with his head lowered, the way the pilot apprentices had taught him. But Carlson grabbed hold of him, aimed a foul blow at his groin, and Norman collapsed like a rolled-up porcupine on top of the dungheap.

"You rotten tramp, you!" he shrieked, no longer able to defend himself with his fists.

Carlsson was brimming over with rage and since he could not call to mind all the invectives he would have liked to use, he placed his knee on the fallen warrior's chest and began slapping his face. Norman spat at him and tried to bite him, and to finish him off Carlsson stuffed his mouth full of straw.

"This time I'm going to scrub your dirty mug clean!" and saying this, Carlsson took a fistful of straw from the dungheap and rubbed his defeated rival's face with it until his nose bled. This final insult opened Norman's mouth. He was sizzling and hissing with rage and his entire vocabulary of taunts and jeers came pouring out in a torrent, right into the very teeth of the victor, who had no means of tying his tongue.

The music had stopped, and so had the dancing; and the witnesses to the fight had made their final comments on the various stages in the battle of words and wits and brute strength without showing any more feeling of concern than they would have displayed had they been watching a slaughtering or a dance game—although some of the older people thought that Carlsson's manner of fighting was not according to accepted old-fashioned rules. But in the midst of this there came a shriek which broke up the crowd and wrenched everybody out of the festive holiday mood.

"He's pulling a knife!" someone yelled, but it was difficult to tell who had yelled this.

"A knife!" the crowd echoed. "No knives! Put away the knife!" And with this they closed in on the two combatants, and Norman, who had succeeded in pulling out his clasp-knife, had it taken away from him and was put back on his feet, after having been torn from Carlsson's unfriendly embrace.

"If you have to fight, boys, fight! But don't use any knives!" With these words the farmer from Svinåker laid the battle to rest.

Carlsson put on his jacket and buttoned it over his torn vest, but Norman walked away with one shirtsleeve hanging down to his knee like a rag. His face was bruised and disfigured, he was dirty and bleeding, and he thought it best to disappear from view so that he wouldn't have to parade his defeat before the girls.

With the proud confidence of being the victor and the stronger, Carlsson went back to the dancing in the barn, and after a nip of brandy he resumed his game of lovemaking with Ida, who received him with ardor and with something akin to admiration.

The dancing kept up like a threshing machine, and it was now twilight. The brandy bottle was passed around ever so often, and soon nobody paid much attention to what was going on next to them. When therefore Carlsson and Ida stole out of the barn and started for the fence by the paddock, nobody bothered them with any insinuating or impudent questions;

but just as the girl had climbed on the steppingstone and Carlsson stood at the top of the fence, he heard the old widow Flod's voice cutting through the half-darkness, although he could not see her.

"Carlsson! Is that you, Carlsson? Then come and dance a dance with your haymaking partner!"

But Carlsson did not answer. Crouching down, he sneaked off as furtively as a fox, farther and farther into the paddock.

The widow Flod had seen him, however, and not only him but the white kerchief which Ida had fastened round her waist in order to protect her dress from the farmhands' sweaty hands. After calling to him once more without getting an answer, she pursued him, straddled the fence and was inside the paddock. The spot where there was a tunnellike depression in the earth, over by the hazel bushes, was submerged in total darkness, and all she could see was something white, which faded away in the murkiness and finally sank to the bottom of the long tunnel. She was about to run after it, but at that very moment she heard other voices over by the fence. One was a heavy masculine voice, the other was more sonorous and tinkling, but both voices were subdued. As they came closer, they reached a whisper. Gusten and Clara clambered over the fence, which gave a creaking sound under the youth's somewhat unsteady steps; and, helped by two sturdy arms, Clara hopped to the ground. The widow Flod hid herself in the bushes, and she saw them march past her, their arms wound about each other, tripping the light fantastic as they went, humming and singing and kissing each other—just as she herself had once upon a time danced and sung and exchanged kisses.

Now a creaking sound came again from the fence, and, jumping over it like a bullock, came the young man from Kvarnö with the girl from Fjällång at his heels. Lingering for a moment at the top of the fence, her face flushed from the dancing and with a forlorn smile that showed a mouthful of gleaming teeth, she petulantly lowered her outstretched arms and clasped them behind her head, pretending she was about to fall; and then—panting and puffing, she broke out into an unrestrained laugh and, with distended nostrils, she threw herself limply into the boy's arms and was received with a long, smacking kiss. Then he carried her in his arms into the darkness.

The old woman crouched behind the hazel bushes and saw couple after couple coming and going, and coming back again—just as when she was young, and the fire of days now past flamed up again after having slumbered under the ashes for two years.

While this was happening, the sounds from the fiddle gradually died down. It was now past midnight, and the red glow of the morning sun could be seen rising almost imperceptibly above the treetops in the north; the sound of voices, mingling in a murmur, coming from the barn, became increasingly dull and lethargic, and a few isolated cheers from out in the meadow indicated that the dancing had broken up and that the haymakers were now getting ready to depart; and the widow Flod had of course to make her appearance and bid them goodbye.

When she had passed through the hollow, into which the light of dawn was beginning to enter so that one could discern the greening foliage, she caught sight of Carlsson and Ida high up on the hillside, clasping each other by the hand as if they were about to gallop off in a polka. Conscious of the humiliation she would suffer if she were to meet someone here in the green underpass, she turned about and scrambled over the fence to go back to the farmhouse before the visitors had left for their homes. But on the other side of the fence she ran headlong into Rundquist who, when he saw her, clapped his hands in utter consternation and the old woman covered her face with her apron lest he be a witness to her shame and mortification.

"Well, may the Lord bless me, if it ain't our Auntie who's been out in the green grass, too! Well, well—so you can't trust the old ones no more either! . . ."

The widow Flod didn't hear the rest. She all but flew to the farmhouse, where everybody had been looking for her, and was received with prolonged cheers, with handshakes, expressions of thanks for the food and drink, and repeated farewells.

And when all was quiet again and the delinquents —barring a few who could not be found—had been summoned in from paddock and field by an *ahoy,* the widow took to her bed. But she lay awake a long time and she kept listening—listening for Carlsson to go up the stairs to his room.

Chapter

4

THERE ARE RUMBLINGS
OF A WEDDING,
AND CARLSSON LOOKS FORWARD
TO A HARVEST OF GOLD.

The hay had been stored away, rye and wheat had been harvested, the summer was over and it had been a profitable one.

"That devil has luck with him in all that he does," said Gusten about Carlsson, who not without reason was given credit for the growing prosperity.

Herring were running and all the men except Carlsson were out among the skerries while the Professor's family was getting ready to go back to the city for the opening of the opera season.

In addition to his other chores, Carlsson had taken on the job of packing their belongings, and all through the day he went about with the pencil behind his ear, quaffing ale in the kitchen, in the dining room, and on the porch, seating himself on top of the kitchen table, on the sideboard, and on the porch bench. After having fallen heir to a discarded straw hat and a pair of worn-out canvas shoes, he annexed a pipe, some cigars that had been left behind, a cigar-holder, empty bottles and packing boxes, pots, jars and fishing rods, nails, corks, and twine—everything that could not be taken along or that the family had no further need of.

The crumbs that fell from the rich man's table were

numerous, and almost everyone shared the feeling that the departing guests would be sorely missed— from Carlsson, who would now be losing his sweetheart, on down to the hens and the pigs, which henceforth would no longer be receiving their Sunday repasts from the fine folk's kitchen. The ones to grieve least were Clara and Lotten. Forlorn, notwithstanding the fact that they had been treated to many a good cup of coffee when they delivered the milk, both girls could not help but feel that a new spring was about to dawn for them, now that fall had come along and removed their formidable rivals from the local love-market.

When the steamboat arrived that afternoon and put in to take the professorial family aboard there was great excitement on the island, for this was the first time a steamboat had landed there. Carlsson took command of the landing maneuvers, spouting orders in all directions, while the captain tried to steer his boat alongside the pier. But this time Carlsson found himself on ice that was too thin, for anything pertaining to the business of the sea was a closed book to him; and at the very moment when the throwing-line was being cast ashore and he proudly wished to exhibit his dexterity for the benefit of Ida and the Professor and his family, a coiled mass of rope landed from above on top of his head, knocking off his cap so that it fell into the water. Trying to grab simultaneously at both rope and cap while they were in flight. his foot caught in a loop. He danced around a few times and hit the ground, showered by a torrent of invectives from the captain, and jeered and laughed at by the hands in the forecastle. Ida turned away, irritated that her hero should have behaved so blunderingly, and on the verge of tears of humiliation on his behalf.

She bid him a curt goodbye at the gangplank and quickly turned to leave. But when he persisted in holding on to her hand and wouldn't let go of it, trying to make plans for next summer, to talk about how they would write to each other and to get her address, the gangplank was suddenly pulled from under him and he was pitched forward so that his cap, which he had fished out of the water soaking wet, was plastered on his neck. At the same time, the mate yelled at him from the bridge: "How do you expect me to back out while you are holding on to that rope? Let go of that tail-end of yours, you . . . !" Another shower of invectives rained down upon the unfortunate lover before he was able to get the rope clear of the mooring post. The steamboat backed away, down toward the inlet, and Carlsson—behaving like a dog who sees his master going off without him—started running along the shore, hopping from rock to rock, stumbling over roots and stumps and stubs, in an attempt to get to the high rocky point where he had hidden his shotgun behind an alder bush so that he could fire a farewell salute to his beloved. But that morning he must have got out of bed on the wrong side, for just as the boat passed and he raised the shotgun to fire it in the air, the shot missed fire. He threw the gun on the grassy ground, pulled out his handkerchief and started waving, and then ran up and down the shore, flourishing his blue cotton handkerchief, hurrahing and blowing, puffing and panting —but no sign of any reply came from the boat, not a hand moved, not a handkerchief fluttered in the air.

His Ida had vanished! Unquenchable in his optimism, he sprang in a frenzy over cobbles and rocks, took a leap into the water, dashed through shrubs of alder, ran headlong into a fence, plunging halfway through it so that he scratched his hands—and then, at last, just as the boat was about to disappear out of sight on the other side of the point, he found himself by a reed-filled creek, and he threw himself recklessly into the water, waved his handkerchief again, and broke into a final, desperate *hurrah!* The stern of the boat moved slowly behind the pines, and then he saw the Professor waving his hat in farewell as the boat steamed further into the cove, the blue and yellow Swedish flag with its posthorn emblem trailing behind, only to be glimpsed once more for a fleeting moment between the alders. That was the last that could be seen of the steamer, except for the long trail of black smoke which hovered over the surface of the water like a mourning veil and darkened the sky.

Carlsson sploshed out of the wet onto the shore and then retraced his steps to the spot where he had thrown down his shotgun. He gave it a venomous look as though he were facing her who had been so faithless to him; and he shook the touch-pan, inserted a new cartridge, and fired.

When he returned to the pier, the whole ludicrous scene came back to him. He saw himself doing his acrobatic dance on the pier planks, like a circus clown or like some jack-in-the-box at a country fair; he heard the raucous laughter, the abuse and invectives; and he recalled to mind Ida's cold and embarrassed look and her handshake when he bid her goodbye. He could still smell the gaseous fumes drifting into his nostrils from the smoking funnel and from the oil and grease in the engine room, the odors of food being fried in lard in the galley, and of the fresh oil paint on the outside plating. The steamboat had come out here to his future kingdom, bringing with it city folk who had showed only contempt for him and who in one swift second had catapulted him from the ladder on which he had already climbed quite a few rungs. What was still worse—and here he swallowed hard—this floating monster had now carried away his summer joy, his happiness. He stood staring for a few moments into the water, which the paddle-wheels had churned up into a regular mudbath, whose surface was studded with patches of soot and oil. The oil patches formed into mirrors, blazing in all colors of the rainbow like an old windowpane. In just a few brief minutes the monster had contrived to empty itself of every imaginable kind of filth and rubbish, littering and soiling the clear, pale green water with beer corks, eggshells, lemon peels, cigar butts, used matches, scraps of paper, all of which became playthings for the alburns and gudgeons. It was as if all the gutters in the city had drained themselves of their waste out there, vomiting up its dregs and pollution at one and the same time.

For a moment he was overcome by gloom and he reflected on the fact that if he seriously intended to capture his beloved Ida, he would have to pursue her to the city, would have to be content with its narrow streets, its courts and alleys, its gutters and slums. For it was in the city that the pay was high, and the clothes grand, where you found gas-lit streets and fine shopwindows, girls with ruffles and frills, lace cuffs and button boots—the city had everything to entice and tempt him. But, at the same time, he also hated the city for there he would be among the least wanted. His provincial dialect would make him the target of leers and grins and scoffing, his coarse, rough hands would be useless for any sort of skilled work, and his wide and varied experience and insight into things would go to waste. Nevertheless he would have to consider taking that step, for Ida had told him that she would never marry a farmhand; and he saw no prospect of ever having a farm of his own. . . . Yet, why couldn't he?

There were ripples on the surface of the water in the inlet, and a cool wind that gradually increased stirred up the water so that it started splashing against the piles of the pier, broke up and scattered the refuse and filth, and cleared away the clouds in the evening sky, so that it was bright again. The soughing of the alders, the lapping and dabbling of the waves, and the bumping of the boats brought him back to reality;

and with the gun on his shoulder he started for home.

The path led him up through the hazelbushes over a knob of rock, and towering above it he saw still another rock face of gray stone, covered with pines. It was a spot he had never seen before.

Out of curiosity he climbed up between the ferns and wild raspberry bushes, and soon found himself standing on a flat surface, where a landmark had been erected.

In the setting sun he saw the island stretched out before him in a bird's-eye view, with its woods and fields, farmhouses and meadows; and in the distance lay holms and islets and a whole belt of rocks extending away into the open sea. It was, indeed, a considerable slice of the good earth, and all this—trees, water, and rocks—could be his if he but cared to stretch out his hand, only one of his hands, and drew back the other hand which was reaching for the vain things in life—a path that would surely lead to nothing but poverty. He certainly needed no tempter to stand at his side and implore him to get down on his knees and worship the glorious sight he saw before him, painted rosy red by the bewitching rays of the sunset—the azure-tinted water, greening woods, and golden fields blended with the red color of the farmhouses into a rainbow which would have cast a spell on a far less intellectual and perceptive person than a farmhand.

The deliberate disdain shown by his fickle one when she, within the space of five short minutes, had been faithless enough to forget her last spoken promise to wave him a farewell had infuriated Carlsson. His feelings had been wounded as though he had been subjected to a lashing of jeers and taunts by overbearing, villainous city folk; and enraptured at the thought of the fat of this land, the abundance of fish in the surrounding waters, and the comfortable farmhouses, he made his resolve—he would go home and make a last attempt, or two, to test the heart that had been so fickle and faithless and which, perhaps, had by this time forgotten him completely. And when that was done—then he would help himself to whatever he could, short of stealing.

When he came back to the hillside and saw the big house standing there deserted, the shades drawn, and straw and empty packing boxes littering the outside, he felt as if a slice of apple were stuck in his throat. After gathering his mementos of the now departed summer guests in a sack, he stole up to his room in the attic, trying to make as little noise as possible. When he had secreted his treasures under the bed, he seated himself at the writing table, took out paper and pen, and made ready to write his epistle.

His first page was one long gushing stream of words, emanating partly from his own mental storeroom, and partly borrowed from the *Chronicles* of Afzelius and from *Swedish Folk Songs,* which he had perused at the home of a farm overseer in Värmland and which had made a lasting impression upon him.

"Dear Beeloved Frend!" he started in. "Alone I sit in my littel room an I am missing you something ter- ribbel Ida I'll never forget its just like yesterday when you come out here Ida. it was when we was sowing the springtime rye and the cuckoo was cuckooing in the bullokk paddock and now we have fall so the boys is after herring out in the skerries. I wouldnt be caring so much about it if you Ida haddent gone away and woodnt say faretheewell to me with a handwaive on the steembote as the Proffesor was so terrible kind to do from the deck in the behind when he come to the point. its empty like a hole tonite after you Ida and so it makes my sorrow heavy to bare. do you remember Ida the prommiss you prommissed to me at the haymaking danse—do you Ida???? I still have the memmery of that prommiss in my head and heart just

as if I had written down it and I can tell you Ida one
thing and that is that I *can keap my prommissess* and
that is what *evrybody* aint able to do but never mind
and I dont care what people do to me but she who I
lov I dont forget thats all I want to say."

The first pangs of parting had now been laid to rest
and a feeling of bitterness began to set in. Soon, however, came the fearful apprehension of unknown
rivals, the temptations of the big city with its famous
Berns' Restaurant where the music was intoxicating
and where gay young blades gathered in the evening.
And realizing how powerless he was to prevent what
he conjured up with dread—the Fall of his Eve—he
turned to nobler and loftier feelings, and in no time
old memories from his days of Bible peddling began
squirting out of his brain. He turned grandiloquent,
stern, and moralistic—a punishing avenger through
whom Another (with capital A) spoke, merely using
him, Carlsson, as his mouthpiece:

"When I think about you Ida being singel and
alone in the jungell city of turrmoil and having
noboddy no more to lean on an proteckt you and to
turn away the danger and temmtation from you Ida
when I think about all the favorrabel times for sinning and distrucktion and evillness what leeds you
from the strate and narow path with a light foot then
I feal a stitch in my heart I feal like I had done wrong
before God and Mankind for leaving you Ida in
the nets of sinfullness I would have been just like a
Father to you Ida and Ida you could have fellt safe in
old Carlssons hands like a real Father . . ."

When Carlsson came to the words "father" and "old
Carlsson" he was stirred to profound sentimentality
and his thoughts turned to the last funeral he had
attended.

". . . a Father what allways overlooks things and has
forrgivness in his heart and on his lips. Nobody knows
how long old Carlsson" (he had already fallen in love

wih the phrase!) "is permited to wander uppon this earth. who can tell if his days aint allreddy reckoned like the water dropps in the sea or the stars in the Heavven—it may bee that before you know he'll bee lyin there like dry hay—an then maybee *somebody* will want to dig him up out of the dust and earth—somebody who dont beleeve Itll come to pass. but let us hope and pray that he bee still sound of Boddy when the Day comes that flowers will bee found all over and the turtell-dove will be heard in our land—then it would be a trooly wondrous time for *many a one* what is now sighing and complaining and wanting to join with the psalmist in singin. . . ."

Here he had forgotten what the psalmist did sing and had to go looking for his Bible in the chest with his belongings. But there were well over a hundred psalms to choose from, and Clara had already yelled out the call to supper, so he had to pick one haphazardly:

"Thou crownest the year with thy goodness; and thy paths drop fatness. They drop upon the pastures of the wilderness: and the little hills rejoice on every side. The pastures are clothed with flocks; the valleys also are covered over with corn; they shout for joy, they also sing."*

When he had read it through, he found that it gave a happy picture of the advantages of pastoral life in comparison with life in the city. And as this was the tender spot, he resolved to leave his epistle as it was and to let the half-uttered hint speak for itself.

That done, he cogitated on what else to write. He felt hungry and tired and could not conceal from himself the fact that when all was said and done, it mattered little what he wrote, for Ida would undoubtedly be lost for him before next spring came around. And so he signed himself "Sinceerly your Faithfull and

* Ps. 65:11.—A.P.

Devotedest Carlsson," and started down to the kitchen to devour his supper.

It had now grown dark and there was a wind blowing. The widow Flod seemed restless, and she came over and seated herself at the table, where Carlsson had lighted a tallow candle and had sat down by himself. The girls moved about in silence, going expectantly from the stove to the table and back again.

"You'd best have a drink of brandy tonight, Carlsson," the old woman began. "I can see you need it!"

"Why, yes, I sure had a job getting all them things on board," Carlsson replied.

"I guess you'll get a little rest from now on," the widow commented as she went to get the hourglass. "It sure is blowing something dreadful tonight, and it's veering over to the east. I wonder how the boys is getting on out there with their nets tonight. . . ."

"Well, that's something I can't do nothing about. . . . I ain't responsible for the weather," Carlsson snapped. "But next week it's got to be fine, for then I'm planning to go to the city with the fish-well to talk with the fishmonger myself."

"Oh—so-o? You plan to do that?" came from the widow with some trepidation.

"Yes. I don't think the boys get a good enough price for the fish. I have a notion something is wrong somewhere—wherever it can be." The widow Flod kept fidgeting and suspected that Carlsson had other errands in town besides selling fish.

"H'm!" she said. "I hope you're going to be polite and go and see the Professor, ain't you?"

"Yes, I suppose I will if I have time. They forgot to take one of the baskets to keep the bottles in. . . ."

"Terrible nice folks they was, I can say that. . . . Don't you want another nip, Carlsson?"

"Thank you, Auntie. . . . Yes, they was nice folks, and I think they'll be coming back here—at least that's what I understood from Ida." He spoke Ida's

name with obvious pleasure. His very way of uttering
it was fraught with conceit and superciliousness. The
widow Flod could not but feel her inferiority, her
hopeless deficiency, and her cheeks began to glow, her
eyes showed fire. In a whisper she said to him: "I
thought it was all over between you and Ida, Carlsson?"

"Oh no, we're not finished by a long shot," Carlsson
fired back at her, promptly aware of a tugging at his
line and feeling that he had put his hook into something.

"You mean to get married, then?"

"I suppose we will, when the time comes—but first I
have to find a job."

The old woman's face, full of lines and furrows,
twitched and she kept plucking at her apron with her
worn hand, like a person sick with fever tugging at the
bedsheet.

Finally she took courage and asked in a dry, trem-
bling voice: "You're thinking of leaving us, then?"

"I'll have to go some day, I guess," answered Carlsson, "for sooner or later a fellow likes to be his own.
. . . And to be wearing yourself out for others is something you don't do for nothing."

Clara had just put the porridge on the table, and
Carlsson suddenly got the mischievous notion to tease
her.

"Say, Clara, ain't you girls going to be afraid of the
dark tonight, being alone in your beds, now that the
boys ain't here? Don't you want me to come and keep
you company, eh?"

"No, there's no need of that," Clara retorted.

For a moment there was silence in the kitchen. Outside, the wind could be heard tearing through the
treetops in the woods, wresting the leaves from the
birches, shaking the fences, threatening to pull down
weathervanes and eaves. From time to time a gust of
wind forced its way down the chimney and blew

smoke and sparks from the fireplace coping so that Lotten had to cover her mouth and her eyes with her hand. And when there was a sudden lull in the wind, the waves could be heard pounding against the rocky point to the east. All at once the dog started barking out on the hillock; then the barking diminished and gradually grew fainter as though the dog were running to meet someone in the distance, either to welcome him or frighten him away.

"Go out and see who it can be, Carlsson, won't you?" said the old widow, and Carlsson promptly got up.

When he had come outside and stood in the doorway, all he could see was a darkness so thick that it was impenetrable to the bare eye, and the wind swept around his head with a force that made his hair dance like dried pea stalks. He called to the dog, but the barking now came from away over in the spring meadow and sounded like a bark of friendly recognition.

"People coming to see us at this hour of the night," he said to the old woman. "I wonder who it can be? I guess I have to go and take a look. Hey, Clara, light the lantern and let me have my cap."

Clara handed him the lantern and his cap and, pushing against the wind, he trudged in the direction of the meadow; then, guided by the barking, he reached the clump of pines which stood between the meadow and the shoreline. The dog was no longer barking, but amidst the soughing and crackling and creaking of the pine trees he now heard the sound of ironshod heels against the rocky ground, the snapping of branches, broken off by someone trying to find his way in the dark, a plop now and then in pools of water, and the whining of the dog, with a string of oaths as an accompaniment.

"Hey! Who's there?" Carlsson bawled out.

"It's the Pastor," groaned a rusty voice in reply; and

simultaneously the sharp, sudden contact of an iron
heel with a cobble set off a regular firework of sparks.
And out of a thicket tumbled a short, thickset, and
befurred man with a rough, jowly, weatherbeaten
face, decorated with wildly untamed gray sidewhiskers
and animated by a pair of sharp, piercing eyes that
peered out from under eyebrows that looked almost
like overhanging moss.

"You certainly have some damned hellish roads out
here on this island," the Pastor growled as a greeting.

"Well, God Almighty, if it ain't the Pastor himself
who's out in this here weather what ain't fit for dogs!"
bellowed Carlsson, reverently returning his spiritual
guide's divinely profane greeting. "But where did you
leave the boat?"

"We came in the fishing-boat and Robert got her
safely tied up at the pier. But let's go to the house so
we can get inside, for the wind cuts right through you
on a night like this. So let's get going—march ahead!"

Carlsson went ahead with the lantern, the Pastor
followed in his wake, and the mongrel followed the
Pastor. Ever so often the dog would make little excursions into the bushes, on the trail of a black grouse,
which had just taken to its wings and saved itself by
flying into the inner reaches of the bog.

The widow Flod came outside and stood on the
hillside to meet the approaching beam of light, and
when she saw it was the Pastor, she was pleased and
bade him be welcome.

He had been on his way to the city to sell his catch
of fish when the storm broke out, forcing him to seek
shelter for the night. He cursed and swore that the
delay might prevent him from disposing of his fish,
since "all the demons in the world were out to sea,
itching to rape it of every living thing!"

The old woman wanted to bring him into the living
room, but instead he headed straight for the kitchen,

preferring to sit near the open hearth where he could get dry. The light and the warmth, however, seemed to cause him some discomfort, for he made wry faces, screwing up his eyes and grimacing as though he were not quite awake. All the while he struggled to get out of his wet boots of dubbed leather, and at the same time Carlsson tried to get him out of his old gray-and-green reefer, made of coarse wool and lined with sheepskin. And before long the Pastor was sitting in a thick woolen fisherman's jersey and in his stockinged feet at a corner of the big table, which the widow had cleared and made ready with the coffee things.

Anyone not knowing Pastor Nordström would ever have guessed that this inhabitant of the skerries held a religious post; to this extent had his thirty years of devotion to the guidance of souls in these outer skerries changed the once quite genteel and polished young divine, who, following his ordination, had come out there from Uppsala. Because of his incredibly meager salary he had been forced to augment it by income from fishing and farming; and if the proceeds from the sale of fish and farm products were not sufficient for his needs, he was obliged to appeal to his parishioners' goodwill and generosity, which he had found it was necessary for him to keep alive by means of social graces adapted to his surroundings. The goodwill, however, consisted chiefly in an extra cup of coffee and divers offerings of certain strong fluids which had to be downed on the premises. Consequently it could not add anything to the welfare and material blessings of the parsonage, but might on the contrary have a detrimental effect upon the beneficiary's physical and moral wellbeing. Furthermore, since the skerry folk—either because dearly bought experience in times of distress on the sea had taught them that God only helps those who help themselves, or because they had a native inability to see any connection between a sudden strong easterly wind and the Augsburg Confession—were unable to derive any benefit from the little wooden chapel they had put up, church attendance frequently suffered. For in order to get there, long distances had to be covered either by rowboat or sailboat, and the latter often ran into untoward winds and could not reach its destination. Thus churchgoing had acquired more the character of country-fair, where one could meet old acquaintances, close deals, and hear official announcements and proclamations read. The Pastor was the only local authority with whom the islanders came in contact, for the sheriff lived a long distance away on the mainland and was never resorted to in any differences of a legal nature. Such issues were invariably settled between the contesting parties by butting heads with each other or over a jug of brandy.

The Pastor had, as mentioned, been on his way to the city with his fish-well, and there he had hoped to sell his catch of fish. But on the way, a storm had suddenly come up, and he had been driven off course by the wind and the waves.

With his shotgun well tucked away in a cowhide case, and with a box of food, and a prayer book in a sealskin bag, the Pastor, feeling wet and miserable, had now come inside into light and warmth. And, after rubbing his eyes, he was at last seated at the coffee table. Not a trace of Latin or Greek could possibly be imagined in this figure of a man—a cross between farmer and seaman—sitting there with the light from the fire and two tallow candles falling upon him. His hand, which had once been white and delicate, and in his youth accustomed to nothing harder than turning the leaf of a book, was now barklike and tanned, with liver-colored blotches from salt water and sun, rough and callused from rowing, and from tiller and sheets; his nails were worn-down and misshapen, with black edges from contact with implements and the soil; his pierced earlobes sprouted hairs galore that choked up the ear passages and were adorned with small leaden hoops as a remedy for

catarrh, inflammation, and excretions. From an improvised leather patch pocket on the outside of his
woolen jersey hung a lock of hair to which a watch key
of some sort of yellow metal and a cornelian were
attached; the water-soaked woolen socks exhibited
holes from which the Pastor's big toes protruded—a
sight he seemed intent on keeping in the dark, judging by the continuous and sinuous wriggling maneuvers of his feet under the table; the jersey had turned
a golden brown from sweat at the armpits, and the fly
of his pants stood ajar for lack of the required number
of buttons.

He produced a pipe from his pants pocket, and
while Carlsson and Mrs. Flod watched in reverential
silence, he tapped it against the edge of the table so
that ash and stale tobacco dropped to the floor, where
they took the shape of a small molehill. But when he
tried to fill his pipe, his hand fumbled, went hither
and thither and all around it, and the two onlookers
began to evince concern.

"Ain't you feeling well tonight, Pastor Nordström?
—I'm afraid you ain't feeling so well, I'm afraid. . . ."
Mrs. Flod finally broke in.

The Pastor raised his sagging head and his glance
drifted toward the beams in the ceiling as though he
were looking for his questioner up there.

"I?" he asked as he spilled a pinch of tobacco
outside the pipe. Then he shook his head as if to say
he would prefer to be left alone, and after that appeared lost in melancholy thought, which seemed to
have no definable substance.

Realizing what was ailing his Reverence, Carlsson
whispered to the old woman: "He ain't sober." And
with a feeling that he ought to take a hand in the
matter, he seized the coffeepot, poured some coffee
into the pastor's cup, placed the brandy bottle alongside it, and, with a deferential bow, asked him to help
himself.

The old clergyman raised his gray head and gave him a withering look, as if he would have liked to scare the life out of him. Pushing aside the cup in repugnance, he spat out:

"Is this your home, you churl?" And then, turning to the widow, he said:

"Give me a cup of coffee, Mrs. Flod!"

After that he sank into deep silence. Perhaps he thought of the days of old, when things were different, and meditated on the fact that people in general were continually growing more insolent and shameless.

"Damned menial!" he spat and sputtered once more. "Go outside and help Robert find the way!"

Carlsson tried to take refuge in flattery but was promptly put in his place by the Pastor's imperious question:

"Do you know where you belong?"—and Carlsson disappeared through the door.

"Have you your herring-nets out?" he bombarded the old widow, who was trying to think up some excuse for the farmhand after the Pastor had braced himself a little with a few sips of coffee.

Mrs. Flod opened her sluices and exclaimed:

"Dear me! Why, yes—we have! And all the sweep-seines too. Who ever would have dreamed at six that we'd have a storm before night! And I know Gusten! He'd go to the bottom of the sea before he'd let the nets lie out there on the reefs all night!"

"Bah! You needn't worry about him!" the Pastor consoled her.

"Don't say that, Pastor Nordström! I don't care so much about them nets, even though they do cost a lot of money—so long as only nothing happens to the boy, I . . ."

"I don't think he'd be fool enough to try hauling in the nets in this kind of weather, with a heavy sea such as tonight on top of him."

"Oh yes—that's just what you can expect of him for

you see he takes after his father, and he was always so pernickety about everything what was his. And Gusten would sooner lose his own life than letting them nets be lost."

"If that's the way he is made—why, then, Mrs. Flod . . . then not even the devil himself could help him! Besides, the fishing is good out there right now. We were out by the Al Rocks a day or two ago, and with six warps we hauled in nearly five hundred herring."

"Well, was they well fed? I mean—was they fat?"

"I should say so—fat as butter. —But now, Mrs. Flod —tell me, what is all this gossip I hear about your thinking of getting married again? Is there any truth to it? Is there?"

"Oh, bless my soul, Pastor Nordström! Is that what they're saying? Well, I must say it's something awful the way people talk once they gets started!"

"Well, well, it doesn't make any difference to me," continued the Pastor, "but if what they say is true about your planning to marry your new farmhand, then I feel sorry for your son Gusten."

"Oh, nothing's going to happen to Gusten, and there's many a young fellow what's had a worse stepfather, I can tell you."

"Oho, so then it *is* true, after all, I see. Is the fire in the old body still burning so fiercely that you can't control yourself any longer, eh? Oh well, that's the way of all flesh, hee-hee-hee-hee!"

"Will the Pastor help himself to another nip," said the widow, breaking into his chuckle. She was beginning to feel uneasy about the amorous turn the conversation was taking.

"Thanks, Mrs. Flod, that's very kind of you! Thanks! I think I'll take it straight this time. But I have to think of getting to bed, too—and I don't suppose you have made up a bed for me yet?"

Lotten was commissioned to make the bed in Carlsson's room in the attic, after it had been decided that Carlsson and Robert were to sleep in the kitchen.

The Pastor yawned widely and loudly, rubbed one itching foot against the other, while his hand flitted across his forehead to his bald pate as if to brush away and put to flight worries and griefs too heavy for words.

All through this, his head sank by fits and starts in short, abrupt flicks and jerks toward the table, where his chin finally found a resting place.

Aware of his condition, the old woman stepped over to him, cautiously put her hand on his shoulder, patted it gently, and in a beseeching voice said to him:

"Dear Pastor! Couldn't we have a few words this evening before we creep into bed? Give a thought to the old widow with her boy out on the water tonight!"

"A few words, you say. . . . Certainly! Let me have the Book, then—you know where I keep it—in the box with the food!"

The widow went to the sealskin bag and took out a black book with a gold cross on the cover, which the Pastor often used as a sort of traveling case, from which he would dispense invigorating and stimulating drops to invalids and elderly women. And full of piety —as though a piece of the Church itself had been brought into her lowly home—the widow picked up the mystical book with both hands as carefully as if she were carrying a loaf of bread hot from the stove, pushed the Pastor's coffeecup to one side, wiped the table with her apron, and laid the sacred pages in front of the afflicted and overloaded head.

"Dear Pastor Nordström, there's the Book," said the widow, in whispering competition with the wind, thundering down through the chimney.

"Good, good," mumbled the Pastor, as if he were talking in his sleep. At the same time he stretched out

his hand without raising his head and groped about
for his cup of brandy, thereby sticking one of his fingers into the ear of the cup and upsetting it, so that
the precious fluid spilled out in two rivulets on the
greasy table.

"Oy, oy, oy," wailed the widow, quickly getting the
Book out of the way of the wet, "this will never do!
The Pastor needs sleep, and we must get him to bed!"

But the Pastor was already snoring, his arm resting
on the tabletop with his middle finger ludicrously
stretched out, as though pointing toward some undis-
tinguishable goal momentarily out of reach.

"How in the name of heaven will we ever get him to
bed?" the worried Mrs. Flod wailed to the girls, without having the slightest notion of how to rouse the
sleeping preacher and knowing only too well what an
irascible temper he could exhibit if he were awakened
after having had a few drinks. And to let him remain in
the kitchen was inadvisable because of the presence of
the girls there; nor could he be permitted to stay in
the living room with the widow—there just would be
no end to the gossip then. The three females circled
him like mice trying to bell a cat, but not one of them
seemed to have the courage to take the first bold
step.

While this was going on, the fire had died out, and
the wind was squeezing in through the windowpanes
and the leaky walls. The old Pastor, sitting in his
stockinged feet, must have been affected by the cold
and the draft, for all of a sudden his head shot up in
the air, his mouth opened wide, and he gave out three
eery shrieks, sounding like a fox giving up the ghost,
which made the three women jump, shaking in their
shoes.

"I must have sneezed," said the Pastor and got up
and moved like a sleepwalker to a sofa near the window. There he sank down, stretched himself out on

his back and, with his hands folded across his chest, fell asleep again with a long, drawn-out sigh.

All hope of getting him out of the living room had now evaporated, and neither Carlsson nor Robert—both of whom had meanwhile come in—were courageous enough to interfere with his sleep.

"Watch out for him! He'll hit you!" This enlightening piece of information was given by Robert, together with this suggestion: "Just give him a pillow and throw a quilt over him—then he'll sleep there until morning."

Old Mrs. Flod took the girls with her into the living room, Robert was given a berth up on the loft in the storehouse, and Carlsson went to his room in the attic. Then the lights were extinguished and the kitchen became silent.

And soon everybody in the farmhouse lay more or less soundly asleep.

The following morning when the cock crowed and Mrs. Flod got up to wake the Pastor, both he and Robert were already gone. The storm had subsided somewhat, bleak, white autumn clouds were driving in toward land from the east, and the sky was a bright blue. At about eight the old widow began her pilgrimage down toward the eastern point to see if she could catch sight of a boat out in the cove. In the channel between the islands a reefed square sail loomed up, only to disappear and then come within sight again. The steel-colored sea was still heaving and tossing, and the rocks in the far distance, tinted by the atmosphere, gave the impression of being a mirage against a seamless backdrop—as though they had floated up through the water to the surface and were in the throes of turning into night mist. In creeks and inlets and on the rocky points young mergansers lay paddling or resting; and as soon as they caught sight of a sea eagle about to swoop down dangerously on

them from the sky, they dove, only to come up and
again start their paddling on the water so that it
sprayed and spumed in all directions. If the widow
saw the seagulls suddenly take to their wings out on
one of the rocky islets and if she heard them screeching, she thought: "Here comes another sail!"—and a
sail did come, but all of them steered a course away
from her island and went either north or south.

A cold wind was blowing, and both the wind and
the white clouds were a strain on her eyes; and so she
trotted back into the wood, tired of waiting in vain.
She took to picking lingonberries, for she had to do
something, and she put them in her apron. She had to
do something to drive away her anxiety. After all, her
son was her dearest possession, and she had not been
half so upset and worried on that night when she had
stood by the paddock fence and watched another dim
hope vanish in the darkness. But today she felt the
boy's absence more deeply than ever, for she had a
premonition that he might not be with her for long.
What the Pastor alluded to last evening, together with
common gossip, had sparked the fuse, and any moment now there could be an explosion. Just who
would get his eyebrows singed was still a matter for
conjecture, but there could scarcely be any doubt that
somebody would be burned. With these thoughts she
slowly jogged along, bound for home, and came to the
slope where the oaken tree stood. Suddenly she heard
the buzzing of voices from down by the pier, and
peeping between the leafed branches she saw people
mulling about near the boat shed, all of them talking
at the same time, back and forth, all trying to be
heard, arguing and bickering. Something had happened while she had been away from the house—but
what?

Her anxiety incited her curiosity, and bracing herself she strode down the hill to see what was going on.
When she had come as far as the meadow fence, she

saw the stern of the fishing-boat. They had come home, then—why, they must have rowed around the island! Norman was giving a running account of what had happened in a steady voice:

"He plunked to the bottom like a stone—and then he come up again. But then death hit him straight through the left eye—and it looked just like when you put out a light."

"O Lord Jesus! Is he dead," screamed the old woman, and she almost flew across the fence; but no one heard her, for Rundquist took up the funeral oration in the boat in loud tones:

"And then we got the grapnel-iron into him, and when the fluke catched him in the back, he . . ."

The widow Flod had come down behind the drying ground where the nets were hanging, but she could not get through; and there she saw as through a dark glass all the inmates of the farm in all sorts of positions, crouching, bending over and crawling around a gray-speckled body that was lying on the bottom of the fishing-boat. She gave one scream after another, trying desperately to get under the nets, but the bark floats got entangled in her hair, and the sinkers kept flinging blow after blow at her, as though trying to scourge her.

"What in the name of heaven have we got in the flounder nets?" bawled Rundquist, who suddenly noticed that something alive was caught in them. "Well, may heaven help us, if it ain't the missis herself!"

"Is he dead?" she shrieked at the top of her lungs. "Is he dead?"

"Dead as a dead dog!" came from Rundquist.

The widow untangled herself and tore down to the pier. She saw Gusten lying bareheaded on his belly in the fishing-boat—but he was not dead—he was moving —and underneath could be seen a huge, hairy creature.

"Is that you, Mother?" Gusten greeted her without turning around. "What do you think of our catch?"

The widow's eyes opened wide when she beheld a fat gray seal whose hide Gusten was in the throes of flaying.

It wasn't every day that they caught a seal, and the meat was edible, the trainoil would grease many a pair of boots, and the skin would probably bring at least twenty crowns. But the winter herring catch was still more crucial to them, and the widow, not seeing even a tail of one in the boat, became quite dejected; and forgetting both the safe return of the prodigal son and her surprise on first seeing the seal, she started to upbraid the boy:

"Well, but what about the herring?"

"Well, they wasn't so easy to get at," Gusten gave as excuse, "and besides, you can always buy herring, but it ain't every day you can catch a seal."

"Well, that's what you always say, Gusten, but I think it's a shame to be out there three whole days and then come back and not bring home no fish. What do you think we are going to have to eat all through the winter?"

But no one showed any sign of being willing to sustain her in her complaint, for they had all had more than enough of herring, and no matter what you said, meat was meat—except for the fact that just now neither herring nor meat interested them half so much as the hunters' stories of their odd adventure at sea.

Here was a chance for Carlsson jealously to hook himself onto a piece of the bait, and he broke in with: "Yes, and if we didn't have no farmin', we'd be gettin' nothin' to eat!"

That day seine-hauling was forgotten, for the big washing-boiler was to be put on the stove for the trainoil cooking; much frying and cooking went on in the kitchen, and one cup of coffee after another was drunk. The skin was hung and stretched on the south wall of the barn in evidence of the great victory at sea and was exhibited and orated about for the benefit of any and all within earshot; everyone was invited to put his finger in the holes where the shots had entered, and all had to listen to how the pellets had penetrated, how the seal had clambered up on the rock, what Gusten had said to Norman at the moment the gun was about to be fired, and, at the very last, how the wounded creature had behaved in its death throes when "the thread of life was cut off."

Carlsson's heroic stature was considerably decimated during all this, but he was secretly forging his steel; and when the seining was over, he sat down at the tiller of the boat with his fish-well and sailed to the city with Norman and Lotten.

When Mrs. Flod came down to the pier to welcome the travelers home from the city, Carlsson was so unusually friendly and soft-spoken that she could not help noticing that something must have happened.

When supper was over, he was invited into the living room to give an account of the money he had received for the herring, and after that was done the widow asked him to tell her all about his trip. Carlsson seemed reticent and in no mood to talk. But the old woman was persistent and wouldn't let him go until she had squeezed some information out of him.

"Well, now, Carlsson," she kept milking him, "I suppose you was up to the Professor, I suppose?"

"Well—I stopped in for a minute or two, of course," Carlsson answered reluctantly. It was evident that he did not relish recollecting the visit.

"Well, how was they?"

"Oh, they asked to be remembered to everybody here on the farm, and they was certainly polite and treated me to breakfast. And they sure live in a terrible elegant *department,* and we got along just fine."

"An' what did they give you to eat what was good?"

"Oh—they give me lobster—and mushroom—and

then they give me some stout, to swallow it down with."

"And tell me, Carlsson—did you see the girls there, too?"

"Oh, sure," was Carlsson's straightforward answer.

"And I imagine they was like they always was, I imagine?" They probably were not, but that chapter would have given the old widow too much pleasure, so Carlsson preferred to keep his mouth shut on that precise point and to go around it.

"Oh yes, they was real nice, and we went to Berns' Rest'rant and listened to the *orkester* playin' music, and then I treated them all to cherry cobblers and san'wiches. We had a real good time, we sure did."

But Carlsson's city visit had in reality been anything but a pleasure to him and had turned out quite differently from his embroidered tale. First of all, Carlsson had been received by Lina in the kitchen and been treated to a bottle of beer at the kitchen table. Ida had not been at home. Then the Professor's wife had come out into the kitchen, had casually greeted the visitor and asked Lina to order a lobster as they were expecting a guest that evening; and then she had left. When Carlsson and Lina were alone again, Lina became a little formal in her attitude toward him, but while they sat there exchanging a few brief words now and then, Carlsson managed to get out of her the information that Ida had received his epistle and had read it aloud one evening when her steady beau was there and the three of them were sitting drinking stout in the maids' room while Lina peeled the mushrooms. And they had all roared with laughter, guffawing until they were almost prostrated when Ida's beau twice read Carlsson's outpourings of love with deep solemnity, in a loud ministerial voice. His reference to himself as "old Carlsson" and his "last moments on this earth" they thought the funniest parts of all; and after having chuckled over the pas-

sage about "temptations and the straight and narrow
path," Ida's boy friend—who drove a beer delivery
wagon—had proposed that they all go out and face
temptation at Berns' Restaurant—and so they had all
gone there and been treated to a cherry cobbler and
sandwiches.

Perhaps it was Lina's account of what had actually
happened that was responsible for stirring up his feelings, muddling his mind and jumbling his memories
until he was totally confused, or perhaps he desired so
intensely to be in the shoes of Ida's beer delivery man
that he simply placed himself in the agreeable role of
host, and vicariously substituted himself for the — to
him unknown — lobster-eating boy-friend, gulped
down his stout, and gorged himself on Lina's mushrooms. Whatever the truth may be, Carlsson told the
story the way he did, and it had the effect he wanted it
to have, which to him was the main thing. And, having done that, he felt sufficiently secure in going to the
attack. The two boys were out in the skerries, Rundquist had gone to bed, and the girls' work was over for
the day.

"What's all this gossiping what's going on here-
abouts all over the place? I hear it everywhere I go,"
he started in.

"What is it they're gossiping about now?" the old
woman inquired.

"Oh, it's the same old babble—about you and me
thinking of getting married."

"Faugh! Such talk's been going round for a long
time now."

"Well, but it ain't right for people to be making up
stories what ain't true. It just goes against my sense of
justice," Carlsson put in like a fox.

"Why—what in the world would a nimble, healthy
young fellow like you want with an old crone like
me?"

"Well, I don't think years got nothing to do with it,

so far as that goes. For I want to tell you this, Auntie
—that for my part, if I ever *should* be thinking of
getting married, it wouldn't be with a young hussy
what knows nothing and ain't able to do nothing. . . .
For you see, Auntie, to be lusting after the flesh, that's
one thing—and being married, that's something else
again. The lust of the flesh, what comes from sinning
in this vale of tears, makes wedlock go up in smoke;
and solemn vows and promises ain't much better than
a chew of snuff when somebody else comes along what
can treat to a cigar. You see, Auntie, I am made this
way, that if I was to marry somebody, I'd be forever
faithful to her through thick and thin. That's the way
I am and always have been, and if anybody says anything different, he's a liar."

Mrs. Flod pricked up her ears and began to suspect
a snake in the grass.

"Oh, but what about Ida? Ain't nothing serious
going to happen between the two of you?" she inter-
rogated him.

"Ida—oh well, she'd do in her own way, I guess. . . .
All I got to do is to give her the nod and she'd jump at
the chance of getting me! But I can tell *you,* Auntie—
she ain't got the right kind of mind—she's got worldly
ways and is full of vanity; and I got a fear she's like to
stray from the straight and narrow. And then, you see,
I ain't so young no more, I tell you, and I ain't got no
hankering to be fooling around with women no more.
. . . Yes, I can tell you straight from the heart that if I
ever *should* be thinking of taking a wife, it'd be somebody what's older and more sensible—somebody what's
got the right kind of mind and disposition. You see—
well . . . you know it ain't easy for me to find just the
right words to say it—but maybe you'll understand me
anyhow, Auntie, for I know you got the right kind of
mind for it. . . . Yes, for you got understanding, and
good sense, Auntie."

Mrs. Flod had to take a seat at the table in order to

be better able to grasp Carlsson's circumlocutious hemming and hawing and to be ready to say *amen* once he had spit out the momentous word.

"Yes—but tell me, Carlsson," she said, picking up a fresh thread in the skein, "have you never thought about the widow at Åvassa? She's sitting there all alone and would like nothing better than to get another man."

"Faugh! Her! Heavens—no! I know her, of course, but she ain't got the right kind of mind, for let me tell you, Auntie—the only thing what would make me want to marry a body is the kind of sense she's got, and her disposition. And money and fine clothes and grand manners and what's on the outside don't cut no figure with me, for I ain't built that way; and nobody who knows Carlsson right, can testify to anything else!"

The subject now seemed to have been gnawed at from every corner, and somebody would have to put in the last word while there was still time.

"Well—who have you been thinking of, then?" asked the widow Flod, boldly taking a step forward.

"I've been thinking and thinking . . . you think here and you think there . . . I ain't been thinking about nobody at all yet; if somebody has—let that body speak! I keep my mouth shut, so that it ain't going to be said that I have led somebody on, for that's not the way I'm built."

By this time the old widow had almost lost her bearings, and so she had to feel her way once more.

"Yes, but Carlsson dear, if you still have Ida in your thoughts, you can't be going around thinking about somebody else and be serious about it, can you?"

"H'm!—that brazen she-fox! Why, I wouldn't take her if you was to throw her at me! Oh no, I want somebody what's better than her—somebody what owns at least the clothes on her back. And if she should be owning something else besides, there wouldn't be no damage done. And it wouldn't make no difference to me one way or the other. For that's the way I am, and that's the kind of character I got!"

At this point there had been so much threshing back and forth and in every direction that there was some danger that they might get stuck in the mud, if the old widow didn't give a push.

"Well, Carlsson, what would you say if you and me was to get tied up together?"

Carlsson threw both hands in the air in a forbidding gesture as if he, brimming with moral indignation, was eager to dispel at once any suspicion that he had harbored such a sordid and covetous thought.

"Oh no, never! That could never be!" he protested. "Let's never talk no more about anything like that, let's not even think of it! Why, there'd be no end to what people would be saying—that I'd taken you for your money. But I'm not that kind—and what's yours ain't mine. No, no—we ain't never in this world going to talk no more about that! Promise me that, Auntie, and give me your hand on it"—(here he stretched out his hand to her)—"that we'll never talk about this here thing no more! Give me your hand on it!"

But the old widow didn't want to give him her hand on it; she wanted to explore the matter to its very utmost.

"And why shouldn't a body talk about it—about something what might just as well be? I'm getting on in years, you know that, Carlsson, and Gusten ain't grown enough to take hold of the farm. I need somebody what can be standing by my side and be helping me. And I know, too, that you don't want to be toiling and wearing yourself out and worrying for others and get nothing out of it. And that's why I see no other way out than for you and me to get married. Let folks talk—they babble and tattle anyway—and if you ain't got nothing in particular 'gainst me, I can't see nothing what could stand in the way. Tell me, Carlsson, just what is it you got against me, Carlsson?"

"I ain't got nothing against you, Auntie—why, no—what makes you think that? But I don't like that Satan's prittle-prattle behind your back—and, besides, there is Gusten—and he ain't going to like us for it, nohow!"

"Faugh! If you ain't man enough to handle Gusten, I can take care of him. I ain't so young no more, but I ain't that old either. And I don't mind telling you, Carlsson, just between the two of us, that . . . well, I don't have to take no backseat for no she-fox when it comes to . . ."

The ice was now broken, and a series of plans and ideas as to how to break the news to Gusten and how to make arrangements for the wedding, and all the other things that go with it, flooded their brains.

These proceedings lasted many hours—so many that the old woman had to put on the coffeepot and bring out the brandy bottle; and it was long after midnight and even a little longer before they were over.

Chapter

5

THERE IS QUARRELING
ON THE THIRD SUNDAY OF THE BANNS.
CARLSSON AND THE WIDOW FLOD
GO TO COMMUNION,
AND BECOME MAN AND WIFE—
BUT LEAVE THE BRIDAL BED UNSLEPT IN.

That nobody is more virtuous and noble than when dead and nobody more miserable than a fellow getting married was something Carlsson would soon find out. Gusten had been barking like a hungry gray seal, had brawled and stormed for three days in a row while Carlsson had gone away on a brief trip, giving a business-deal as a pretext. Old man Flod was dug up out of his grave, was turned inside out, and was declared to be the finest and noblest human being that had ever been born, whereas Carlsson's past was scrutinized to the seams like old clothes and found to be full of patches and stains on the inside.

It came to light that he had been both a railroad bum and a Bible peddler, that he had been discharged from three jobs and had left another without giving proper notice, and it was also said—this, however, was merely an unconfirmed rumor—that he had been taken to court once for having assaulted someone. All this was held up to Mrs. Flod's face, but the flame in her breast had been lighted, and quickened by the prospect of an end to her widowhood, the old woman seemed to be on the threshold of a new life, mustered fresh energy and a will to do whatever she wanted to do, no matter what stood in her way.

The hostility to Carlsson had its roots primarily in the fact that he was an outsider, an interloper, and that he would now, through marriage, come into possession of this tract of land and its shore and fishing rights, which they — as native-born islanders — had come to regard, in a certain sense, as their common property.

As the widow had been left with a jointure and could be expected to live many years yet, the chances of the son's coming into possession of the farm were meager; and after the marriage his position would differ little from that of a menial for he would be dependent upon the goodwill of the former farmhand who, as his stepfather, would be his legal guardian. Small wonder, then, that the newly demoted one flew into a rage and fired some pretty sharp words at his mother, threatening to write to His Majesty the King, to make a court case out of it, and to have the future stepfather kicked off the island. His temper reached its boiling point when Carlsson came back from his little outing attired in the late old man Flod's black Sunday coat and sealskin cap, which—during the couple's first tender moments together—the widow had duly presented him with as a dowry.

Gusten said nothing but he bribed Rundquist to play one of his pranks, and one morning, as they were about to sit down to breakfast, Carlsson found a towel covering a pile of something or other at his place at table. Not suspecting that anything unpleasant was hidden there, he picked up the towel and found himself sitting face to face with all the treasured junk he had collected in a sack after the Professor's departure and then hidden and forgotten under his bed in the attic. The display included empty lobster and sardine cans, mushroom jars, an empty stout bottle, a multiplicity of corks, a cracked flowerpot, and many other keepsakes.

Carlsson turned green in the face but he didn't know whom to pounce on. Rundquist stepped into the line of fire, averting an explosion by explaining that in that part of the country, it was a common custom to play such pranks on someone who was about to get married. As luck would have it, Gusten came in just after Rundquist had said this, and expressed astonishment that the junkdealer had come around so early in the fall, since he usually did not come until just after New Year's. And to make matters still worse, Norman piped up with the intelligence that no junkman had been there and that the collection was made up of Carlsson's mementos of Ida which Rundquist wanted to tease Carlsson with, now that their love duet was over.

This remark led to an exchange of sharp words, after which Gusten took off to see the Pastor, whom Gusten persuaded to postpone the wedding for six months because of the doubtful character of Carlsson's past. This was a fly in the ointment for Carlsson, who promptly tried to make up for it as best he could by seeking requital for himself in several minor ways. In the beginning he had taken his new position with ostentatious solemnity; but when this attitude evoked snickers he decided to go upon another tack and act his rôle in a more playful and jocular manner, at least in his intercourse with the folk on the farm. And in this new character he succeeded tolerably well, except for Gusten, who kept up a deadly subversive, acrimonious warfare and showed no signs of being conciliatory.

In this manner the winter passed in the usual quiet, monotonous way with the felling of timber, cutting of logs for firewood, net-making and ice-fishing, with interludes in the form of card playing and coffee drinking, with a nip of brandy, a Christmas party or two, and hunting the long-tailed duck. And then spring came again. The return of the migratory eider duck tempted the Hemsö natives out to sea, but Carlsson put all hands to work on the spring sowing in order to be able to look forward to a rich harvest— which would be needed to fill the inroads the wedding festivities would make on the stored grain. For it was intended that this wedding should be a thumping one —one to be remembered for years to come.

Along with the migratory birds came the summer guests, and the Professor continued nodding his nod of goodwill as he had done all through the previous summer. He still thought that everything was *schön,* so much the more so because Hemsö was soon to be the scene of a wedding. Fortunately, Ida was no longer with the family. She had left the professorial ménage in April and was said to be preparing for her impending marriage. The girl who had taken her place was not especially prepossessing, and Carlsson had far too many irons in the fire to want to get mixed up with anyone in an amorous way. Now that he held all the good cards in his hand he did not care to risk losing the game.

The request to have the banns published was made on Midsummer Day. The wedding was to be held during the interval between the haymaking and the harvesting, since at that time there was always a slackening off in the farm chores as well as in the fishing and hunting.

Once the request had been made, an unpleasant change became noticeable in Carlsson's behavior and disposition, and the widow Flod was the first one to get a taste of this. Although the two had been living together from the day they became engaged—as was the custom among country folk in those days—Carlsson, who was still under suspicion, had taken pains to adopt a conduct and attitude conforming to the demands of the situation. But the moment that the danger was over, he stuck his nose in the air and revealed his claws. This, however, had no effect on his future wife who was equally confident of herself. On the contrary, she, too, began to show her teeth—what few she had left—and when the banns had been read from the pulpit for the third time, the two went at each other tooth and nail.

Everybody on the island, with the exception of Lotten, had traveled to the little church to be given communion. In accordance with custom, they took the smallest boat so that, should it be necessary to take to the oars, they would have to exert themselves as little as possible. Because they were taking along a batch of chub, several pounds of candles for the sexton, a variety of clothing (in case of getting splashed), a box of food for themselves, and in addition, sails, oars, bailers and buckets, hassocks and footboards, there was not much room left in the boat.

As was the habit on such occasions, they had had a more substantial breakfast than usual and had treated one another to the contents of various jugs and bottles. The sun beat down, and because of the heat nobody wanted to do the rowing. This led to a quarrel among the men, for none of them wanted to arrive at church dripping with sweat. The women interceded; and when they came into the inlet where the church was situated and heard the sound of the bells, which they had not heard for well over a year or longer, the argument was laid to rest. The bells were ringing the first call to mass, so there was no need to hurry. Therefore the widow Flod proceeded to the parsonage with the fish. The Pastor sat shaving himself and was in a crusty mood.

"We'll have rare visitors at church today, with the folks from Hemsö here!" was the way he greeted her, at the same time scraping the mixture of hair and soap lather off the razor blade onto his forefinger.

Carlsson, who was carrying the fish offering, was sent out to the kitchen, where he was treated to a long drink.

Their next visit was to the sexton, who got his candles, and where Carlsson was given another drink.

At last they all met again on the slope by the church where they looked over the horses that had brought the wealthier farmers to the church, gazed at the inscriptions on the gravestones, and greeted people they knew. Mrs. Flod paid a brief visit to the grave of her late lamented husband, while Carlsson stepped out of sight for a moment. And then the bells started to ring again, bing-bonging in the steeple, and it was time for the congregation to crawl inside. But the Hemsö folk had had no pew since the old church had burned to the ground, so they had to stand in the aisle. It was frightfully hot, and they felt ill at ease in the sizable interior. They began to sweat out of sheer embarrassment and looked like culprits in a lineup. It was eleven o'clock before they came to the psalm-singing that preceded the sermon, and the Hemsö natives had changed from one position to another, had crossed and uncrossed their legs and shifted their weight from one foot to the other at least forty times. The sun poured in, blazing hot, and the sweat ran down in beads from their foreheads, but they stood there as if stuck in a vise. Not a shady spot was in sight anywhere, and they were so jammed together that they could not have budged if they had wanted to. Then the church caretaker appeared and put up hymn number 158 on the hymnal board. The organ wheezed out a prelude, and the sexton started the singing with the first verse. The congregation sang with animation and visible delight, for everybody took it for granted that the sermon would follow immediately after verse one. But then came verse two, and then number three.

"You don't mean to tell me the Pastor is having us

sing all them eighteen," Rundquist whispered to Norman with trepidation.

But that was exactly what the Pastor meant to do. And in the open door to the sacristy could now be seen the irate countenance of the Reverend Nordström. He stood defiant and challenging, looking out over the congregation as if he were determined to rake them over the coals and give them a good wigging, now that he had them in his grasp.

And so all eighteen verses were sung, and it was eleven-thirty before their shepherd appeared in the pulpit. But by this time they had been tenderized and softened, the starch had, in fact, been taken out of them so completely that their jaws hung down on their chests and they went to sleep standing up.

But their dozing didn't last long—for in a moment the Pastor would give a sudden shout which brought the sleepers back to consciousness with a start. Their heads would pop up, and they would stare at their neighbors like imbeciles, as though they were asking if the church was on fire.

Carlsson and his intended had taken up places so close to the pulpit that they couldn't possibly retreat to the door without causing comment. The widow Flod was completely exhausted, her buttonboots, which were too tight for her feet, pinched her abominably, and more and more as the midday heat kept increasing. From time to time she turned around and gave her beloved an imploring look as if pleading with him to take her in his arms, carry her down to the water, and throw her in.

But Carlsson—his feet encased in old man Flod's roomy horse-leather boots—was so carried away by the Pastor's divine words that he had nothing but a punishing look of intolerance for the restless one. Some of the others had gradually succeeded in dropping astern and had taken refuge beneath the organ loft where the air was a bit cooler and the sun didn't beat down on them. There Gusten caught sight of the fire-extinguisher and he promptly sat down on it, putting Clara on his knee.

Rundquist steadied himself against a pillar, and Norman stood next to him when the sermon commenced. And their shepherd certainly did not beat around the bush—he excoriated them in words that everybody could understand, and his sermon lasted one hour and a half.

The text he had chosen for the occasion was the parable about the wise and foolish virgins. As this was a topic which had no bearing on the males, they went to sleep in unison, some sitting down in the aisle, others standing, others hanging onto whatever they could find.

After half an hour of this, Norman gave Rundquist a jab in the side, as he stood doubled over, his hand on his forehead as though indisposed, and with his thumb pointed in the direction of Clara and Gusten, calling attention to the flaming lovers on their love-seat on top of the fire-extinguisher. Crazy Rundquist turned cautiously toward them, and his eyes opened in a wide stare as if he had just beheld the Evil One himself. He shook his head and leered a leer as if to say that he had taken due cognizance of the shocking scene. For there he saw Clara, her tongue hanging out of her mouth and her eyes closed as if she were having a nightmare, while Gusten had his eyes fixed in a stare upon Preacher Nordström in the pulpit and looked as if he were swallowing every one of his words and were straining to hear the sands in the hourglass run out.

"Oh, but that's terrible!" said Rundquist in a whisper, slowly backing up and cautiously feeling his way with his heel in order not to make any clattering sound against the brick floor. But Norman had already divined what was in Rundquist's mind and quick as an eel he had slunk out of the church into the churchyard, where Rundquist also appeared shortly. Then the two escapees steered their course down to the boat.

Down there a cool breeze was blowing from the sea, and they soon helped themselves to some of the food they had brought along. As furtively and noiselessly as they had slipped out, they now sneaked back into the church on tiptoe; and there they saw Clara sound asleep in the lap of the snoozing Gusten, whose arms were entwined round her waist and so high up that Rundquist thought it only proper to lower them a few notches. During the course of this operation, Gusten came back to consciousness and took a new hold on the maiden, as though someone were trying to snatch his fair booty away from him.

It was still another hour before the sermon came to an end, and then there was another half-hour of hymn-singing before Communion started. The sacramental means of grace was accepted with profound emotion. Rundquist shed tears, but old Mrs. Flod who—when the ceremony at the altar was over, tried to obtain a seat in a pew and was turned away—almost started a quarrel. And so she spent the final half-hour outside the caretaker's pew, resting on her heels as though the brick floor were burning the soles of her feet; and when Pastor Nordström announced the banns, she nearly went out of her mind because everybody was staring at her.

Then, at long last, it was over and everybody made a dash for the boats. The widow Flod couldn't wait any longer and pulled off her pinching buttonboots as soon as she had received the congratulations of the churchgoers. She carried the boots in her hand all the way down to the boat, and when she got there she promptly stuck her feet into the water and started to berate Carlsson. Then they all went ravenously for the food, and when it was discovered that the pancakes had mysteriously disappeared, there was growling. Rundquist spoke up and said he thought they must have been left behind, and Norman assumed that someone must have helped himself on the way to the church, thereby throwing a nasty suspicion upon Carlsson.

Finally they were seated in the boat, but just then Carlsson remembered that he was to bring back a barrel of tar that had been stored by the Pastor. The women started to remonstrate, saying that under no condition did they want anything like that in the boat because they would get their dresses smeared, but their objections were to no avail. Carlsson went after the barrel and brought it aboard; and then the women fought about who was going to sit next to the dangerous object.

"What do you want me to sit on now," whimpered the widow.

"Pull up your skirts and sit on your behind," Carlsson retorted. He felt that he could afford to be a little more familiar now that the third Sunday of the banns was almost over.

"What was that you said?" hissed the old woman.

"Yes, that's just what I said! Sit down in the boat and let's shove off!"

"Who do you think you are, giving orders on this here boat?" Gusten jumped on him, feeling his honor as a seaman encroached upon.

And with this, Gusten sat down and took the tiller, giving orders to run up the sail and to sheet home. The boat was heavily loaded and there was hardly any wind stirring, the sun was blazing hot, and tempers were seething. The boat crawled ahead like a louse on tarred tree bark; and that the men had been given an extra drink of brandy did not help matters. It was not long before their patience ran out, and after a brief interval of silence, Carlsson broke in and proposed that they lower the sail and take to the oars. But that was not what Gusten wanted, and he said: "Just wait! Wait! Once we're past the rocks, we'll start sailing! Just wait!"

And so they waited. Already they could see a dark

streak of blue out in the gut between the islets, and
they could hear the thumping and breaking of the
waves against the seaward skerry rocks. A strong wind
from the east was coming in and the sail started to
flap; and no sooner had they passed the rocky point
than a squall hit them so that the boat keeled over on
its side. It righted itself again and then made headway
so that the water swirled and eddied in its wake.

This was an incentive for another drink; and that
in turn eased tempers. All the while the boat was
surging ahead at a good speed. But then the wind
freshened, the leeside railing dipped under the water
and the boat sailed along with the wind abeam. Carlsson was terrified. Holding on to his thwart with all his
might, he begged that they heave to and put in a
reef.

Gusten ignored Carlsson's suggestion, and instead
he sheeted home the sail, and the water came rushing
in over the railing.

Carlsson shot up from the thwart like an arrow,
almost insane with fright, and grabbed one of the
oars, trying to put it out into the water; but Mrs. Flod
took him by the tail and resolutely pushed him down
on his seat.

"For the Lord's sake, sit down, man! Sit down in
the boat!" she screamed.

Carlsson sat down, but his face had turned ashen.
He didn't sit still long, however, for he suddenly
jumped up again, this time visibly beside himself,
flapping his coattails and screaming at the top of his
lungs:

"May God have mercy on us! She's leaking, ain't
she?" And all the while he kept flapping his tails.

"Who's leaking?" everybody asked in unison.

"The barrel—the tar barrel, can't you see!"

"Lord Jesus! Oh!"—and now there was a general
uproar with everybody trying to get as far away as
possible from the oozing, trickling tar which was flow-

ing in rivulets and bifurcating in all directions to the swaying of the boat.

"Sit down in the boat—or I'll sail you all to the bottom!" Gusten fumed.

Carlsson stood up again just as a gust of wind lashed the boat. Rundquist, sensing danger, lifted the rear part of his anatomy carefully from the thwart and gave Carlsson a solid smack with such gusto that he landed on the bottom of the boat. It looked as if a fight was in the offing, and the widow Flod became panicky and thought it was about time for her to take some action.

She grabbed her lover by the coat collar and started shaking him.

"What kind of a poor slob are you? Ain't you never been out in a boat before? Can't you act decent—like a man—and sit still in the boat, eh?"

Carlsson became enraged and tore himself loose from her grip but lost a piece of his coat collar in the process.

"Do you want to tear my clothes to pieces, you hag?" he yelled at the top of his voice, hanging his boots on the railing so they wouldn't get tarred.

"What did you call me?" Mrs. Flod hissed back at him, her eyes shooting fire. "Your coat! Your coat, eh? Who give you that coat? Tell me that! You ain't going to call me no hag, you stinking herring spawn, you— what ain't even got nothing worth buzzing about, ha!"

"Shut up!" bellowed Carlsson, who had been punctured in his tenderest and proudest spot, "or I'm like to tell the truth about you!"

By this time Gusten felt things were beginning to go a little too far, so he started yodeling a schottische, in which Norman and Rundquist joined. The venomous exchange of words simmered down, and instead they all turned to devouring the common enemy, Pastor Nordström, who had kept them on their feet for five hours and eighteen verses. The liquor bottle was passed around again, the wind became less variable, tempers calmed down, and when the boat swept into the cove and bumped against the pier at Hemsö, everybody was in good humor.

Preparations for the wedding were now promptly begun; it was to last for three whole days. A pig and a cow were sacrificed for the event; one hundred pottle-pots of liquor were ordered; herring was salted down and spiced with bay leaves; and there was no end of scrubbing, baking, cooking, brewing, frying, and grinding of coffee beans. During all these preliminary goings-on, Gusten moved about with an air of secretiveness. He let the others make the decisions, offering neither suggestions nor advice. Carlsson, on the other hand—if he was not off to Dalarö on some important mission—sat most of the time at the chiffonier-desk, scribbling and calculating, or he busied himself with the many little details for the coming event.

The day before the wedding was to take place, Gusten packed his hunting bag early in the morning, took his shotgun, and was on his way out of the house. His mother woke up and asked him where he was going. Gusten replied that he was going down to the water to see if the chub had come in yet; and with that he left.

But down at the shore he had his boat lying well supplied with enough provisions to last for several days. He had also taken along a quilt, a coffeepot, and a few other articles needed for a stay out in the skerries. He did not tarry making sail, and instead of taking off for the inlets and channels, where the chub was in the habit of seeking out the warm sand of the shallow beaches to "bathe"—as the Hemsö natives used to call it—Gusten set his course straight out between the rocky islets.

It was in the morning of a radiantly clear day at the

end of July. The sky was a bluish white, like the color
of skimmed milk, and holms and islands, skerries and
rocks blended so delicately with the surrounding
water that one could not but wonder whether they
were joined to the earth or to heaven. On the rocky
islet closest to land grew spruce and alder; and among
the reeds at the rock points goosanders, scoters, smews,
and seagulls were resting. Farther out toward the open
sea only dwarfed pines could be seen, and out there
common guillemot and the parrotlike black guillemot
swarmed brazenly about the boat, seemingly in an
attempt to confuse the hunter and divert his attention
from their nesting-places, hidden in the crevices of the
rocks. Still farther out, the rocks decreased in height
and became more barren, and there nature had left
only an occasional pine to hold the nesting-boxes in
which eider ducks and mergansers lay their eggs, only
to have them plundered, or a mountain ash, over
whose crown a swarm of midges would float like a
cloud, moving almost imperceptibly in the wind.

And beyond lay the glittering open sea where the
long-tailed skua carried out its pirate raids upon
terns and seagulls, and where the sea-eagle could be
seen winging its way in dread, tempestuous flight,
hoping to carry aloft a sitting duck as its prey.

It was to this spot—the outermost island in the
skerries—that Gusten now steered his boat. Settling in
a reclining position, with a pipe in his mouth and his
hand on the tiller, he let himself be drifted along in
the mild, southerly breeze; and about nine o'clock he
put in at Norsten. This was a small rocky islet of but a
few acres, and across its middle ran a glen. Only a
couple of baldheaded mountain ash stood among the
rocks, but in the crevices there also grew the luxurious
spindletree with its fiery red berries; and the glen was
overgrown with a thick carpet of heather, crowberries,
brush, and cloudberries, which were beginning to take
on their yellow color. A scattering of juniper bushes

lay flattened against the rock-face as though they had been trampled by human feet; and it seemed as if they were hanging on by their nails lest they be blown away.

It was here that Gusten was at home, really at home. He knew every stone, knew where to find the breeding eider duck, which—even when taking a nip at his pants—let him stroke her feathers. Here he could get a razorbilled auk by putting a forked stick down into a crevice; and then he would cook the bird for breakfast after having wrung its neck. Here was where the natives of Hemsö did their fishing in the open sea just beyond and where they had built a hut together with some fishermen from a neighboring island.

To this hut—in which they would often spend a night—Gusten now wended his way. He found the key in its usual place under the eaves and took his togs and things inside. The hut had only one room, and no windows. It had built-in bunks, one on top of the other, a stone hearth, a table and a three-legged stool to sit on.

After he had put everything away, Gusten climbed onto the roof, opened the smoke-vent, and then climbed down again. When he had done this, he took the matches from their hiding-place underneath one of the beams and made a fire in the open stove where —in accordance with accepted custom—whoever had used the hut last had seen to it that an armful of wood was there, ready for the next occupant. Then, putting a pan of potatoes on the stove, and on top of the potatoes a batch of salted fish, he lighted his pipe and waited.

Having finished his meal, which he washed down with several gulps of brandy, he took his shotgun and proceeded to the boat where he kept the decoys. He rowed out a distance with them and anchored them beyond a rocky point; and having done that, he took up a position in the hunters' blind, which had been put together and camouflaged with stones, twigs, and boughs. The decoys were rocked and tossed about on the long, undulating swell of the sea which broke against the rocks, but there was no sign of eider ducks anywhere.

He waited a long time and grew weary; then he sauntered about among the rocks on the shore, hoping to find an otter, but all he could stir up was some venomous vipers and a hornet's nest about his ears, which happened to him when he walked through bright purple loose strife and withered yellow oatgrass.

He showed no particular eagerness to catch anything, however, and it seemed as though he kept idling about merely for the sake of doing nothing—as an escape from his life at home, or because he found it to his liking to be drifting about aimlessly out here, where there was no one to watch what he was doing and where he could not be overheard.

After having had his midday meal, he lay down in the hut to sleep, and late in the afternoon he took his fishing line and rowed out to sea to try his luck that way. The water now lay still, its surface shining like a mirror; and reflected in the golden highway of the setting sun, the surrounding landscape took on the semblance of shadowlike smoke. All about reigned a silence such as you find on a windless night, and from several miles away he could hear the sharp, metallic sound of turning rowlocks. The seals took their dips into the water at a discreet distance, thrusting up their round-shaped heads, barking and blowing with their nostrils, and then diving in again.

The cod were really hungry for the bait, and he was lucky enough to haul in several white-bellies. With their wide but harmless, gaping jaws they kept yawning for water and made wry faces at the sun when they were pulled up out of the dark of the deep sea and dragged in over the railing.

He had been keeping to the north side of the skerry, and from here the hut was not visible. Night fell before he knew it, and he started rowing back. It was only then that he noticed smoke coming from the chimney of the hut. Wondering what could be the matter, he steered his steps briskly toward the wooden refuge.

"Is that you, Gusten?" came a voice from within, and he recognized it as Pastor Nordström's.

"Well—so it's you, Pastor?" answered Gusten with surprise when he saw the parson seated in the glow of the open fire, frying herring. "Is the Pastor out here by himself?"

"Yes, I'm out here, hoping to catch some cod; but I've been over on the south side—that's why I didn't see you. —How is it that you are not at home, getting everything ready for the wedding tomorrow?"

"Well, you see, Pastor—I ain't going to be at that wedding, that's why!" was Gusten's curt reply.

"Oh, what kind of nonsense is that? What reason could you possibly have for staying away?"

Gusten gave his reasons as best as he could, and the gist of it was that he had two reasons: he wanted to stay away from an event that was sickening to him, and he wanted to shame forever the man who had wronged and offended him.

"Well—but what about your mother?" the parson remonstrated. "Have you no pity for her? Don't you realize the shame it will bring on her?"

"I don't see why I should feel pity for her!" Gusten retorted. "Ain't it much more shameful for me to be getting a rotten scoundrel like him for a stepfather and not being able to take over the farm so long as he's sitting there?"

"Well, my boy—but you see, that's something that can't be changed right now anyhow. However, there

may come a time later on when something can be
done about that. But for the present you must get into
your boat tomorrow morning and go back home. You
have to be at that wedding!"

"Oh no—I ain't going—no, sir! I've made up my
mind to that!" Gusten persisted stubbornly.

The Pastor dropped the subject and started to eat
his herring by the open fire.

"I don't suppose you brought any liquor with you,
did you?" he opened up again. "You see—my wife has
the bad habit of locking up all the intoxicants, so I
often have to go thirsty."

Gusten had, indeed, taken along a supply of what
was poison to the minister's wife, and so the Pastor
was given a generous measure of drinks. As a result he
opened up the sluices and began blathering indiscriminately in confused fashion about the official business of the county, both of a public and a confidential nature. And seated on the rocks outside the hut,
the two watched the sun go down and twilight settle
over the skerries and sea like a melon-colored haze.
The gulls went to sleep on beds of seaweed, and the
crows withdrew to the inner skerries to seek refuge in
the woods for the night.

It was time to go to bed and the midges had to be
chased out of the hut. In order to get them out, the
two men filled their pipes with Black Anchor tobacco
and began puffing away until the hut was full of
smoke. Then they opened the door, and the hunt was
on with twigs of mountain ash. When the chase was
finished, the two fishermen pulled off their coats and
climbed into their bunks after having shut the door
tightly.

"Now you can give me a nightcap," begged the
parson, who had already had more than enough.
Gusten, however, gave him the last unction at his bed-
side, and then they both were ready to go to sleep.

It was dark in the hut, and only an occasional trace

of twilight filtered in through the drafty walls. The midges, however, despite the meager light, found their way to the sleepy pair, who turned and twisted in their primitive bunks in an effort to escape their torturers.

"Oh, this is just too damnably horrible!" the parson finally cried out with a groan. "You are not asleep, Gusten, are you?"

"Sure—I'm sound asleep! —No, I'm afraid we ain't going to get much sleep tonight. And there ain't nothing we can do about it!"

"We have to get up and start the fire again, that's about all we can do. If only we had a deck of cards, we could play a game of *mariage*. I don't suppose you have one, have you?"

"No, *I* ain't got none, but I think I know where the boys from Kvarnö keep theirs," Gusten replied as he climbed out of his bunk. Then, crawling on the earthen floor, he crept under one of the lower bunks and came out with a pack of cards that showed marks of wear and tear.

The Pastor had started a fresh fire, having put a few boughs of juniper on the open hearth and lighted the fag-end of a candle. Gusten put on the coffeepot and pulled out a herring keg which they placed between their knees and used as a card table; and then they lit their pipes, and the cards began to fly, and in that way they passed the time.

"Three fresh cards! —Pass! —Trump!" the men called out, coloring their exchanges of palaver with an occasional oath, whenever a midge suddenly put its bloodletting instrument into a neck or knuckle.

The Pastor, however, seemed to have his mind on something besides midges and cards, and suddenly he stopped in the middle of the card-playing and said:

"Listen, Gusten, don't you think you could give him a lesson that he would remember, without staying away from the wedding? People will think you are a

coward if you stay away—they'll think you are afraid
of a good-for-nothing like him—and if you really want
to vex him and get the best of him, I know a much
better way."

"Well, tell me what you got on your mind—what is
it, Pastor?" Gusten asked. His thoughts suddenly
turned to the refreshments and all the good food,
which he would hate to miss and which would be paid
for out of his patrimony anyhow.

"Why don't you come home in the afternoon—soon
after the ceremony is over—and say that you ran into
trouble out on the sea? That, in itself, would be in-
sulting enough—but then we two, you and I together,
will get him drunk as a fool so that he won't be able
to get into bed with the bride! And then we'll get the
boys to tease him and make him a butt for their jokes!
Don't you think that would be giving him what he
deserves, eh?"

Gusten was beginning to fall in with the idea, and
the thought of having to spend three days by himself
out on the rocky islet and be eaten up by midges so
that he couldn't sleep nights, made him vacillate—
particularly since in his heart he longed to join in the
merrymaking and to have a taste of all the many good
dishes and delicacies he had seen while they were in
the process of being prepared. And so the Pastor conceived an idea of how to carry out the adventurous
plan, and it was accepted by Gusten who was to do his
share in bringing it to fruition. And satisfied with
themselves and each other, they were finally able to go
to sleep at daybreak, after the light of day had stolen
in through the slits and cracks in the door and the
midges had grown tired of their nocturnal polka-
dotting.

That same evening, Carlsson had learned from
some fishermen who had returned from their herring
fishing that they had seen Gusten and the Pastor in

their boats, both steering toward Norsten; and Carlsson promptly conjectured that they were cooking up
some diabolical mischief. He had taken an intense
dislike to the parson, not only because the wedding
had been put off for six months, but also because the
Pastor missed no opportunity to show how little regard he had for Carlsson. In his relations with the
Pastor, Carlsson had been cringing, fawning, and
servile and had tried to gain his favor in devious ways,
but the Pastor had remained incorruptible. Whenever
they were together under a roof anywhere, the Pastor
would always see to it that he had his broad back
turned to Carlsson, he never even listened to what he
said, and the stories he told would always hide an
unmistakable barb against Carlsson.

When Carlsson now heard that the Pastor and
Gusten had been together out in the skerries, he took
it for granted that their meeting had had a definite
purpose. Consequently, instead of waiting for them to
put into effect whatever scheme their clandestine
meeting had produced—and of which he strongly suspected he would be the victim—he hatched a plot
which would stop his adversaries halfway in their con-
spiracy.

It so happened that the boatswain at the coast-
guard station in the district was on a furlough and
had taken a temporary job as bartender and general
helper at Hemsö, where his accomplishments as organ-
izer of public dances and other social entertainments
were known and valued. Carlsson hit the nail on the
head when he thought he could count on his coopera-
tion in playing a prank on the parson; for Boatswain
Rapp had been refused his confirmation papers because of his predilection for chasing after girls. This
delay caused him trouble when he tried to enlist in
the navy, which he therefore could not join until a
year later. And so the two, filled with venom for eccle-
siastics, personally and in general, got together over a

cup of coffee and brandy and schemed to play a joke on the Pastor that he would not soon forget. And it was their mutual opinion that the Pastor should be filled to the brim and be the recipient as well of other diverse little attentions which time and circumstances would dictate.

In this manner mines were laid by each opposing side, and it was a matter of luck which side would gain the victory.

The wedding day came. Everybody woke up tired and out of humor after all the hard work of getting ready, and when the first guests arrived earlier than expected (this because of being unable to calculate the time it would take to come by water, owing to changing wind and weather conditions) no one was there to receive them; and so they had to roam about, looking foolish, on the slopes and hillocks, as if they had not been expected. The bride was still in the throes of dressing, and the bridegroom was running about in his shirtsleeves, busy wiping glasses, uncorking bottles, and putting candles into candlesticks. The living room was decorated with leaves and had been scrubbed, and all the furniture had been moved outside and placed at one end of the house so that it looked as if there was to be an auction. In the yard a flagpole had been erected, and at its top was unfurled a flag with the insigne of the Customs Department, which the district inspector had generously lent for the solemn occasion. A wreath and crown made of lingonberry twigs interlaced with white daisies hung over the living-room door, and on each side of the doorway were leafed branches of birch. In each window stood a lineup of bottles bearing labels in such flamboyant and screeching colors that they gave the effect of a liquor-shop window, shining far out on the hillock—for Carlsson had a predilection for eye-filling and fancy effects. From the soap-green glasses, filled with golden Swedish *punsch,* emanated a sheen as from sunrays; and the golden purple of the cognac glowed like the embers of a coal fire; the protective, silvery capsules over the corks glistened like freshly minted coins, causing some of the bolder young farmers to step closer and gape as if they were gazing into a shop window and had had a foretaste of an agreeable tickling of the palate.

Guarding the entrance and flanking the doorway, like two heavy artillery pieces, reposed two casks, each one holding sixty pottles—the one filled with strong brandy and the other one with near beer; and on either side of these lay stacked up, like pyramids of cannonballs, two hundred bottles of beer. It was a magnificent and warlike sight, and Boatswain Rapp paraded about like a constable on patrol, with a corkscrew dangling from his pants belt, organizing the supplies and munitions of war placed under his command. He had embellished the casks with spruce boughs, which he had hollowed out and then inserted metal stopcocks into them. He was swinging his bunghole hammer like a cannon swab, tapping the barrels now and then, merely to let the guests know that they were by no means empty. Rigid in his parade uniform, which consisted of blue blouse with turned-down collar, white pants, and patent leather hat—the sidearm he had dispensed with for the sake of safety—he inspired great respect in the farm boys. Aside from his job as bartender, he had been given the authority to keep order, avert mischief, bounce troublemakers—if the need arose—and to intercede whenever it looked as though a fight were in the brewing. The sons of the well-to-do farmers acted as if they had contempt for him, but this was from envy, for they were all only too eager to wear a uniform and serve the Crown, but their fear of irascible gunners and lashings from a rope's end or a cat-o'-nine-tails kept them from joining up.

In the kitchen two caldrons of coffee stood on

the open stove, and coffee grinders, borrowed from neighbors, creaked and groaned; sugar loaves were split with an ax and chopped into small pieces, and coffeecake was stacked high on the windowsills. The farm girls ran back and forth between the kitchen and the storehouse, which was stuffed full with meats of every kind, cooked, fried, roasted, and baked, and with bags filled with freshly baked bread. From time to time, the bride would poke her head out of the attic window, dressed only in her nightgown, her false braids dangling about, yelling one moment to Clara, the next to Lotten.

Sail after sail could now be seen steering into the cove, luffing past the shed on the pier, and then laying to at the sound of a shotgun salute, after the sails had been taken in. But it took a while before the arrivals gathered the courage to make for the farmhouse; and so the guests were still roaming about in flocks up and down the slopes.

As luck would have it, the Professor's wife and children had had to go to the mainland to attend a birthday celebration there, and only the Professor was now at home. He had accepted the invitation to be present at the festivities and had also offered the use of his big parlor for the religious ceremony, and his lawn, shaded by oaks, for the coffee party and the supper afterward.

Long planks galore had been laid on barrels and trestles to serve as benches along the tables, which had already been covered with white cloths and set with coffeecups.

On the slope in front of the farmhouse the people now began to gather in small groups. Rundquist— freshly shaved, his hair slicked down with blubber, and wearing a black coat—had appointed himself court jester for the solemn occasion and was doing his best to entertain the guests with barbed quips and remarks, while Norman—who, together with Boatswain Rapp had been entrusted with the firing of the big salute of the day, chiefly by means of dynamite sticks—had withdrawn behind the house, where he was rehearsing on a lesser scale with a moderately noisy small pistol. In exchange for this post of distinction, he had had to forgo the company of his accordion, which was locked up for the day, owing to the fact that the island's favorite fiddler, the tailor at Fifång, had been engaged to play; and this gentleman was exceedingly touchy about any interference in the exercise of his artistry.

And finally came the Pastor, brimming over with a jovial, merry wedding mood, and fully prepared for the usual clowning with the bridal couple demanded by tradition. He was welcomed by Carlsson, who received him at the threshold.

"Well, will you be ready for another visit to church right away?" was the way the Pastor greeted him.*

"Oh, hell, no—there is no hurry about that!" answered the bridegroom without the slightest embarrassment.

"You are sure about that, eh?" the Pastor came back at him, to the amusement of the grinning farmhands. "I have married, baptized, and held church services for women recovering from childbirth—all on the same day—at weddings; but that was for people who were healthy and strong and fit to give a satisfactory account of themselves. —Speaking seriously, however —how is the bride standing up?"

"H'm. There ain't no danger right now, but you never know when something might happen," Carlsson retorted, guiding the Pastor inside and seating him between the wife of the church caretaker and the widow of Åvassa, whom he entertained by talking about weather and fishing conditions.

* The birth of a child not long after the marriage ceremony was not an infrequent occurrence among country folk in those days.—A.P.

At this moment the Professor made his entrance, dressed in tails and white tie, and topped by a black high hat. The Pastor immediately attached himself to him as an equal and a personage and started a conversation to which the two crones listened with wide-open ears and bulging eyes, certain in their hearts that the Professor's brain was crammed full of learning.

Then Carlsson suddenly appeared on the scene announcing that everything was ready, and that they were now only trying to find Gusten so that the ceremony could commence.

"Where is Gusten?" The cry was being shouted back and forth on the hill from as far away as the barn.

But there was no answer. And no one had seen Gusten.

"Oh—I got a good idea where he is," was the enlightening intelligence given by Carlsson.

"And where do you suppose he can be, then?" Pastor Nordström broke in mischievously in a tone that Carlsson promptly took notice of.

"A little singing-bird told me. He told me he'd seen him out at Norsten. And with him was some filthy pig what got him to drink, I shouldn't be surprised!"

"Oh well—then I see no use in waiting for him—if he's got into bad company out there. I must say, though, I think it's not very nice of the boy not to have stayed at home, where a good example is set for him and where he can get guidance. —I wonder what the bride—his mother—has to say? Shall we commence, or does she think we ought to wait a little?"

There was deliberation with the bride, and even though she felt very depressed about Gusten's absence, she was anxious to start the proceedings since the coffee would get cold if they waited any longer. And so the party broke camp and marched up the hill to the accompaniment of a dynamite salute from the rocky hills. The fiddler rubbed his bow with resin and tightened up the pegs, the Pastor enveloped himself in his gown, the bridesmen formed a vanguard, and the Pastor escorted the bride who was wearing black silk and a white veil, and had a wreath of myrtle on her head and was so tightly laced that what was intended to be concealed, protruded only still more. And thus the wedding party moved in procession up to the Professor's to the tune of the creaking, squeaking fiddle and the reverberations of the thundering salute against the rocks.

To the very last, the old woman kept throwing anxious glances over her shoulder, looking for a sign of her prodigal son, and when they were about to pass through the entrance door the Pastor literally had to drag her inside with her nose rubbing against her back. Finally they were in. The guests lined up against the walls as though in formation for a public execution, and the bridal pair took up a position in front of two chairs which—turned upside down—were covered with a Brussels carpet. Pastor Nordström, who had taken out his prayerbook, was fingering his ministerial bands, and was about to clear his throat when the bride nervously touched his arm and asked him to wait. Only a few moments—then surely Gusten would be there. . . .

The silence in the room became almost oppressive. All one could hear was the creaking of boots and the rustling of starched skirts and petticoats. After a few moments this ceased; people began looking at one another in embarrassment, coughed drily—and then there was silence again. At last the Pastor, with all eyes turned on him, said:

"Now we'll begin! We can't wait any longer! If he is not here by this time, he is not coming."

And saying this, he began the ceremony by reading: "Dearly beloved fellow-Christians. . . . Marriage is an institution which has been ordained and consecrated by God himself . . ."

The services had progressed in this manner for several minutes, and the older women, sniffing at their sweet-smelling lavender sachet bags, were already in tears, when all of a sudden a resounding *pop!* was heard outside, followed by the earsplitting sound of glass smashing into smithereens. For a moment everybody pricked up his ears, after which attention was again riveted on the Pastor's oratorical effort, with one exception—Carlsson, who became nervous and restless and cast furtive glances through the window. Then came another *pop-pop-pop*—as of champagne bottles being uncorked—and the boys and young men standing by the door started to titter and snicker and giggle. The disturbance simmered down somewhat, and then the Pastor asked the big question with these words: "Before God the Almighty, who is all-wise and all-powerful, and in the presence of this congregation, I ask you, Johannes Edvard Carlsson: Will you take this Anna Eva Flod to be your wedded wife, to love and to cherish in joy as in sorrow?" But instead of an avowal from Carlsson came another devastating cannonade which interrupted the holy act. There was a crash of glass and flying splinters, and the mongrel began to bark hysterically.

"Who is it who is opening bottles out there, disturbing this holy service?" roared Pastor Nordström, now in a rage.

"Yes—that's just what I'd like to know!" sputtered Carlsson, who by this time was unable to restrain either his curiosity or anxiety. "Don't tell me it's Rapp who is making all this hullabaloo?"

"Oh now—just a minute! Don't accuse me of something I ain't done!" Boatswain Rapp, standing innocently fixed in the doorway, vehemently gave vent to his indignation over having had a finger pointed at him.

Pop-pop-pop! There was no cessation from the mysterious popping battery.

"In the name of Jesus, go out and see what's going on, so that we won't have an accident here and so that we can continue with the ceremony!" screeched Pastor Nordström.

Some of the wedding guests rushed outside to reconnoiter the terrain, and others flocked together around the window.

"It's thé beer!" someone was heard yelling.

"Das pier! Das pier! Das pier is running avay!" exclaimed the German Professor excitedly.

"Why—what an idea—letting the beer lie in the hot sun!"

There, stacked high, lay the beer bottles, cracking and banging away like machine-guns, foaming, fizzing, hissing, and spitting and the froth running all over the grass and the ground.

The bride almost went out of her mind over this unforeseen interruption of the ceremony, which did not bode well for the future; the bridegroom was taunted for not having made better arrangements and was on the point of getting into a fight with the boatswain for trying to shift the blame onto him; the Pastor was angry because the nuptials had been impeded by the beer-bottle barrage, while the young men stood outside on the slope drinking leftovers from the broken bottoms which they just happened to have salvaged during the rescue work—together with a few half-filled bottles that had lost their corks but had not been broken. When the commotion was finally over, the congregation assembled again in the Professor's parlor, this time, however, with less solemnity than before; and after Pastor Nordström had recapitulated the grave momentous question to the bridegroom, the ceremony proceeded with no further disruptions barring a few unsuccessfully repressed giggles from the boys standing in the hall.

And then congratulations were heaped upon the newlyweds, and everybody left the parlor as speedily as possible, eager to get away from the smell of sweat and damp socks, the sweet odors of lavender and withered flower bouquets—and from tears. And now they marched less ceremoniously, setting out for the coffee table.

Carlsson took a seat between the Pastor and the Professor, but the bride was too restless to sit still and kept running here and there and everywhere to see that things were properly served and attended to.

The sun was resplendent on this July evening, and there was laughter and merrymaking and eager chatter under the oak trees. Brandy was freely poured into the coffeecups after the dunking had come to an end, and second and third cups were poured. At the head of the table, where the bridegroom was seated, they drank Swedish *punsch,* without any show of envy by the farmers or their sons.

It was not a drink that was offered every day, and the Pastor gulped down swallow after swallow from his coffeecup.

Today the parson was uncommonly gentle in manner toward Carlsson and toasted him again and again, praised him and showed him the most extravagant attention although at the same time he did not disregard the Professor whose acquaintance was a source of greater enjoyment because he so rarely had an opportunity to meet a cultivated person. But he found it a little difficult to establish contact and meet with him on common conversational ground since music was not his forte; and the Professor politely sought to lead the conversation onto the Pastor's sacred domain, from which the Reverend Nordström was most eager to stay away. The linguistic difficulty these two had in understanding each other contributed to making it impossible to bring them really close together. Aside from this, the Professor—more expert at airing his feelings through music—was averse to engaging in longwinded conversations.

But just then the fiddler, who had found it increasingly difficult to sit unnoticed in a corner, staggered up to the seat of honor, and—his courage visibly fortified by a succession of coffee-and-brandies—proposed that he and the Professor talk music.

"Excuse me . . . I beg your pardon, Mr. Court-Musician," he greeted the Professor, simultaneously twanging on the fiddle strings as a salute to a fellow-artist, "me and you—we belong together, if I may say so, for you see, I'm a fiddler, too, you see, in my own way, of course . . ."

"Get the hell away from here, tailor, and don't be cheeky!" Carlsson snubbed him.

"Sure, sure—excuse me—but I don't see what you, Carlsson, got to do with this! Anyhow, I want you to have a feel of this here fiddle of mine, Mr. Court-Musician, and then tell me if it ain't a fine one. . . . I got it at Hirsch's store in Stockholm where they sell music and I paid forty-two fifty for it cash."

The Professor twanged at the E-string, smiled, and commented amiably:

"Sehr schön! Mutch schön!"

"There you see! It takes somebody what knows—then you find out the truth. . . . But to be talking about art with them people here . . . ha . . ."

This last pronouncement the fiddling tailor had intended to submit in a confidential whisper, but his vocal resources refused to yield to a more delicate shading so that instead he gave vent to his feelings in stentorian tones, and he continued imperturbably:

". . . these damned stupid louts, these peasants! . . ."

"Give the tailor a kick in the pants!" everybody chanted in chorus. "Watch yourself, tailor! You better not get sozzled tonight, or we won't be having no dancing!"

"Hey there, Rapp! You better look after the fiddler! See that he don't get no more to drink tonight!"

"Ain't I supposed to get free drinks maybe? Are you stingy, too, you bastard?"

"Sit down, Fredrik, and take it easy," the Pastor warned the tailor, "or you'll be in for a thrashing!"

But the fiddler had made up his mind to discourse on the art of fiddling, and to further elucidate his claim about his fiddle's superior qualities, he strummed on it, and tootled:

"Listen, Mr. Court-Musician, just listen to them basses! Did you ever hear basses like that, did you? Eh? Don't they sound just like a church organ—like a small organ? Eh? . . ."

"Make the tailor shut up!"

There was movement and excitement about the table, and the general befuddlement became increasingly evident. Then suddenly they heard the cry: "Gusten is here!"

"Where? Where?"

Clara supplied the intelligence that she had seen him on the slope where the wood was kept.

"Let me know when he is in the house," the Pastor requested. "But not before he is actually inside, you understand!"

The toddy glasses had now been placed on the table, and Boatswain Rapp started to uncork the cognac bottles.

"Aren't you going a little too fast with the drinks?" the Pastor interposed, shaking his head in refusal; but Carlsson offered the opinion that things were only going as they should go.

Boatswain Rapp went around slyly urging everybody to clink glasses with the Pastor, and it was not long before he had finished his first toddy and was urged to fix himself another.

Soon he began rolling his eyes and champing his teeth, noisily chewing back and forth, up and down. He scrutinized Carlsson's face as intently as he could in his condition, trying to discern whether the upstart had been raked over the coals yet and been given what Gusten and he had cooked up for him. But he seemed to see things in a mist, and it ended with their drinking a toast to each other.

At that instant, Clara came rushing in, calling out:

"He is in the house now, Pastor Nordström! He is down there now!"

"What the devil is it you are saying, girl? Is he there already?" The Pastor had forgotten who it was they were talking about.

"Who is it who is there, Clara?" everybody asked in chorus.

"Gusten, of course!" answered Clara.

The Pastor got up, went down to the farmhouse, brought back Gusten, and led him to his end of the table. Gusten was shy and looked like a fish out of water. The Pastor drank a toast to him in a cup of Swedish *punsch,* and he was cheered roundly. When this was over, Gusten raised his glass in a toast to Carlsson with a laconic "Good luck!"

This made Carlsson sentimental and he emptied his glass to the last drop, averring that he was very touched to see Gusten, even though he had come late; and that he knew two human beings whose old hearts had been warmed at the sight of him, even though he had come late. . . .

And he ended his oratory by saying:

"And believe me—anyone who knows how to touch old Carlsson in the right spot, he knows where he's got him, believe me!"

Gusten was not carried off his feet, but he invited Carlsson to have another glass with him, just the two of them together.

Twilight set in, the midges started their buzzing around, and chattering was heard everywhere; glass clinked against glass, laughter rang out, and here and there little helpless cries could already be heard coming from the bushes, the sounds broken into by gig-

gling and cheering, boisterous catcalls, and noisy gun-
play under the open sky on this mild summer evening.
And out in the meadows, the crickets were chirping,
and the corncrake croaked its raucous croak.

The tables were now being cleared and made ready
for the festal supper. Boatswain Rapp had borrowed
the Professor's Japanese lanterns for the occasion and
was going about hanging them upon the boughs of the
oak trees. Norman was rushing around, carrying arm-
fuls of plates, and Rundquist was down on his knees
drawing near-beer and brandy, the girls carried in
herring, piled up on cutting-boards, stacks of pancakes, meatballs, and no end of bread and butter. And
when the table was set and everything was ready, the
bridegroom clapped his hands.

"Please step forward and help yourself to a sant-
witch!" was Carlsson's invitation to the guests.

"But the Pastor ain't here? Where's the Pastor?"
broke in the older women who stood on ceremony.
Without the black coat no one was willing to begin.

"And where's the Professor? What's happened to
them? No, no—we could never start eating when they
ain't here!"

Everybody began shouting and ahoying and looking
for the two dignitaries, but to no avail. The wedding
guests stood in droves around the table like ravenously hungry dogs, with a glint of ferociousness in
their eyes, as though they were ready to make an attack; but no one had the temerity to start in, and the
silence became oppressive.

Then Rundquist broke it by asking in his most innocent voice:

"I wonder—could the Pastor maybe be paying a
visit to the outhouse?"

Without waiting for any further intelligence, Carlsson took a promenade to reconnoiter the secret abode,
and—true enough!—Rundquist's amazing power of
divination proved correct, for there—with the door

wide open and each with a newspaper in his hand—sat the Pastor and the Professor in the midst of a spirited debate. On the floor stood a lantern, which had the effect of a footlight cast upon the two dignitaries, each one proudly seated on his throne.

"Excuse me, gentlemen. . . . Excuse me—but the—the santwitches—the santwitches is getting cold, gentlemen. . . ."

"Oh, it's you, Carlsson! Oh, is that so? Well, well—you go ahead and start in—we'll be there in a moment . . ."

"Yes, but—but the folks is all standing 'round waiting, and—and I hope the Pastor don't mind me saying it, but—couldn't you gentlemen try to hurry up a bit? Couldn't you?"

"Run along! Run along with you, Carlsson! We're coming! We'll be there in a minute!"

Not without satisfaction Carlsson got the impression that the Reverend Nordström was a little under the influence of certain strong fluids, and he hastened back to relieve the guests of their uneasiness. He explained that the Pastor was busy preparing himself and would be there shortly.

Some moments later, a rambling lantern seemed to be straggling about aimlessly on the hillside and gradually came closer to the festal table, groaning under the generous spread.

The parson's ashen face soon came into view at the head of the table, and the bride stepped forward with the breadbasket, meaning to invite him to start the supper and so put an end to the long and painful wait. But Carlsson had in mind something entirely different and rapping his sterling silver knife on the meatball platter, he announced in reverberating tones:

"Silence, good people! Silence! Pastor Nordström has something to say to you!"

The Pastor stared at the bridegroom as though he

wasn't fully conscious of just where he was. He dimly observed that Carlsson held a silvery object in his hand—and that brought back to his memory a speech he had given last Christmas with a silver cup in his hand. And so he lifted his lantern high, opened his mouth and spoke:

"My dearly beloved friends! Today—today we are celebrating a glorious day!"

Having come this far, he stared at Carlsson again in the hope that he might provide him with some inkling of what sort of celebration it was, and for what purpose it was being held—for by this time his mind had apparently gone completely blank, and neither time nor space, reason nor judgment any longer existed for him. And the grin on the bridegroom's face furnished no solution to the riddle. He stared far out into distant space in an attempt to find a lodestar to guide him, and noticed the Japanese lanterns in the oak tree. There he found the answer and his inspiration— for in his unsteady condition it looked to him like nothing so much as a giant Christmas tree—and now he had something to go by.

"This joyous festival of Light," he spluttered, "when the summer's sun gives way to wintry cold . . . and the snow . . . (here his eyes rested on the white tablecloth which to his bedimmed eyes took on the appearance of an endless field of snow stretching far into the beyond) . . . when the first snow of winter falls like a bedspread over the muck and dust, the grime and slime of fall, then . . . why—no—I believe you're making fun of me. . . . H'm."

Pastor Nordström turned around and keeled over.

"The Pastor's got a chill," said Carlsson, "and he wants to go to bed. Please start right in and help yourself, everybody!"

The guests didn't have to be asked twice. They made a charge for the heaped-up food and their parson was left to take care of himself.

The Professor had set aside the attic room in the big house for the Reverend Nordström to spend the night in; and in order to give an exhibition of his sobriety, the Pastor declined all offers of help, threatening to thrash anyone who persisted in trying to assist him. Thus, with the lantern dangling at his knees, and bent over as if he were looking for sewing-needles in the dewy grass, he set his sights for a window, from which a light shone. But when he came to the gate, his clothes got tangled up in it, and he hit the gatepost with such force that the lantern was smashed, and he was without a light to see by.

Darkness closed in around him like a sack, and he sank down on his knees, but the light in the window was like a beacon to him and he kept on going in the belief that he was walking in a straight line toward it, although he had the uncomfortable feeling that his black pants were getting wetter and wetter with every step he took; and his kneecaps ached as if they were constantly being pounded by stones.

Finally he grabbed hold of something very large, round, and moist. He groped about and felt something sticking into his hand, like a paper with sharp pins in it or something that felt like it; and he caught hold of a tholepin or some such thing. In the same breath he heard the rushing of water and had a feeling that he was soaking wet. Shaken out of his wits at the thought that he had landed in the sea, he embraced something that gave him support and thought it was the mast of a boat but then found—when a faint glimmer of light struck it—that he was holding onto a doorpost. Then he was suddenly catapulted into an entrance hall, felt his knees knocking against steps going up, and heard a girl give out a scream: "For the love of Jesus! The near-beer! The near-beer!" Given impetus by a bad conscience, he crawled up the stairs, bruised his knuckles on a key, pushed against a door, and was flung into a small room where he saw a bed, wide enough for two and all ready for occupancy. He still had enough strength left to turn down the bedcover and he crept into bed, boots and all, in order to hide and get away from all those who he imagined were in pursuit of him with their shrieks from below. He had the feeling that he was dead or dying, or had flickered out, or gone to the bottom of the sea, and that vast throngs of people were clamoring for near-beer. But now and then he would come back to life, his heart ticking again; then he was dragged up out of the sea, was once more alive, and was standing by the Christmas festal table—only to flicker and be blown out again, like a candle, dead, engulfed by the sea, and sunk. . . .

While this was happening, the evening meal under the oak trees was well under way and was rinsed down with beer and hard liquor in such quantities that the Pastor was completely washed out of mind. And when every bit of food had been devoured so wholeheartedly that platters and plates looked as if they had been both washed and dried, the company trotted down to the farmhouse to dance in the bridal couple's living room.

The bride wanted to send something good to eat up to the Pastor's room, but Carlsson was able to convince her that Pastor Nordström ought to be left alone and that it would be a shame to disturb him; and, besides, it would embarrass him. And so the matter was passed over.

When Gusten saw that Carlsson had gotten the best of his partner-in-crime, he left the minister in the lurch and abandoned himself to the pleasures of the evening, throwing rancor and bad blood to the winds of forgetfulness and befuddlement.

The dancing went like a millwheel, and the fiddler, seated by the fireplace, ground away with his bow, and sweaty backs hung out of the windows, seeking to get cooled off in the fresh night air. But on the slope,

the older folk sat enjoying themselves, breaking into
laughter whenever a shot boomed out, smoking,
drinking, and cracking jokes in the twilight and by
the faint glow from the open kitchen fireplace, which
glittered through the windowpanes, and from the illuminated living room, where the dancing was going
on.

Out in the meadows and up on the hillocks one
couple after another sauntered through the dewy
grass in the glimmer of the starry sky, to put out—to
the scent of new-mown hay and the chirping of
crickets—the fire, which the heat inside the house, the
intoxicating beverages, and the lilting tempo of the
music, had kindled and stirred up in them.

The midnight hours raced by and the sky was
brightening in the east, where a streak of light appeared. The stars withdrew into their heavenly abode,
and Charles's Wain had its thill standing straight up
as if the vehicle had overturned backward: the ducks
could be heard quacking among the reeds, and reflected in the glistening cove were the lemon-tinted
shades of the dawning sun, coming into view between
the mirrored images of the dark elder trees, which
seemed to be standing on their heads in the water and
stretching away down to the very bottom of the sea.
But this picture remained for only a moment, for
clouds—rolling in from the coast—invaded the sky-
line; and there was night again.

And just then shrieking, screaming sounds were
heard from the kitchen: "The *glögg*, the *glögg!*" And
marching in line came the men, carrying a large vat,
from which blue flames of burning brandy cast a flickering light upon the procession, all to the accompaniment of a stirring march fiddled by the fiddler.

"The Pastor's got to have the first glass! Up to the
Pastor!" Carlsson shrieked, not without the hope that
the *glögg* might prove the crowning blow in his pastoral vendetta, and the suggestion was received with

cheers. The procession promptly set off toward the
Professor's house, and the entire flock climbed up the
stairs on legs that were more or less steady. The key
was in the outside keyhole of the door, and the whole
company clambered inside, not without a certain feeling of trepidation that they might be welcomed with
cuts and blows. But inside was nothing but stillness,
and by the flickering blue light from the steaming
glögg they saw that the bed stood empty and was unslept in. A dark premonition of some terrible mis-
calculation took hold of Carlsson, but he did not give
voice to his suspicion; and he dismissed his uncer-
tainty and conjectures with the spurious, fabricated
explanation that he just remembered that he had
heard Pastor Nordström say something about spend-
ing the night in the hayloft in order not to be bothered by the midges. But as it was dangerous to take
the flaming vat near the hay, the idea was dropped at
once, and the marchers made an about-face and
trotted down to the slope, where the burning *glögg*
offering was quaffed.

Carlsson quickly appointed Gusten to take his place
as host, and then took Boatswain Rapp aside and told
him of his dreadful fears. Without being seen by anyone, the two confederates stole up the stairs to the
bridal chamber, taking a candle stump and matches
with them.

Rapp lighted the candle, and in the bridal bed
Carlsson saw a sight that more than surpassed his
very worst fears.

On the white, hemstitched bedpillow rested a
matted, tousled head, looking more like the head of a
shaggy, wet dog, with his mouth gaping wide open.

"Why—did you ever . . . ! What a creature!" Carlsson sizzled, gnashing his teeth. "Who could have
thought the old wretch would have made such a pig of
himself? God have pity—and if the fiend didn't go to
bed with his boots on, too!"

The two were in a quandary. How were they to get the sick man out of the room without having to touch him, without letting the people know anything about it, and—above all—without the bride learning what had happened?

"We have to heave him out of the window," Rapp determined after having pondered the situation. "We'll have to hoist him out with block and tackle and then drag him down to the water! Put out the candle and let's go up to the barn and find a tackle."

They closed the door, locked it from the outside, and took the key with them. Then the two avengers took a circuitous road up to the barn. Cursing and swearing, Carlsson promised that if they could only get the Pastor safely to the ground and down to the water, they would make him an object of ridicule later.

As chance would have it, the cattle-shears were still there after the cow-slaughtering; and when they had taken down the spars and got hold of the tackle and rope, they stole their way back in the same secretive manner to the rear of the little farmhouse, and from there to the gable underneath the Pastor's window. Rapp went and got a ladder and fastened the spars together at their upper ends, spreading them apart at the lower ends, and securing them by means of a lath to the ridgepole. Then he spliced some rope into a loop, attached the block to it, and inserted the tackle. After having done that, he crept back into the Pastor's room, while Carlsson remained below with a boat-hook, ready to start the big adventure.

After Rapp had been laboring for quite a while, his head at last appeared in the window. Puffing and panting, sniffling and snorting, he gave his orders in a muffled voice to Carlsson: "Haul away!"

Carlsson started hauling, and it was not long before a dark body came bouncing out onto the window ledge.

"Keep hauling away! Hard!" commanded Rapp, and Carlsson gave a hard pull. And with a jolt, out came the flabby, inanimate body of the Pastor, stretched to an unbelievable length and looking like a hanged man; and there he dangled on the spars.

"Lower away! Slacken off! Down!" Rapp ordered now. "Get a good grip on the rope!"

But it was too late. Carlsson had already let go of the rope, and Pastor Nordström landed in a heap of stinging nettles; yet he did not utter a sound.

In less than a second, the boatswain was out of the window and removed the ladder and the hoisting apparatus; then he and Carlsson dragged the Pastor down to the washing-barge at the shore.

When they had come down to the water's edge, Carlsson gave vent to his vindictiveness.

"Now, you villain—now you're going to get the bath of your life!"

The water at the beach was shallow but oozy and muddy from the leavings of fish guts, which had been thrown there through the years and had rotted into slime.

Rapp took him by the strap, which he had fastened round his belly, and unceremoniously heaved him into the water.

This brought the Pastor back to life and he gave out a screeching, screaming squeal sounding like a stuck pig.

"Haul him out!" Rapp suddenly gave the command, having become aware that the folk on the hillside had heard the loud squeal and were rushing down to see what was going on.

But now Carlsson went down on his knees and began kneading and seasoning the Pastor with mud and mire, rolling him in the stinking slime, rubbing it into his black clothes with his hands so that every trace of his unfortunate accident was covered up.

"What's going on down there? What's going on?"

the onrushing crowd yelled when they were within earshot.

"The Pastor plopped in the water! Ahoy!" Rapp answered, as he pulled out the shrieking parson.

Now everybody swarmed to the spot. Carlsson acted the part of the magnanimous hero, the good Samaritan, who had saved their shepherd from drowning; he rolled his eyes, effusively lamenting the unfortunate occurrence in his peculiar native dialect, which he always fell back upon when he wished to appear convincing and tenderhearted.

"Can you imagine," he gushed and bubbled, "I was coming along down here—*absoloot* by accident, yes— and then I hear something splashing and rolling about in the water, and I thought it couldn't be nothing but a seal—and then I find it's our own dear pastor! May the Lord save us, if it ain't Pastor Nordström himself lying there, flapping his angel wings, I says to Rapp. And then I says to Rapp, I says: 'Rapp, you run and get a rope, Rapp!' —And then Rapp ran after a rope. But when we got him strapped round the part where he sticks out—then he started screaming like mad! You'd have thought we was trying to castrate him. And look at him! See how terrible he looks!"

Pastor Nordström certainly did look a sight, and the men gazed at their shepherd with something resembling disgust, mixed with ineradicable reverence, and were eager to get him away from there as speedily as possible.

To accomplish the removal, a pair of oars was made to serve as a stretcher and upon this the parson was laid. And on the shoulders of eight sturdy men he was carried in procession to the barn, where he was to be renovated and given a change of clothing.

The fiddler, who was thoroughly tipsy, got the idea that it was some sort of festal parade coming along, and immediately hugged his violin and joined the

parade, striking up: "Make way there, make way there
for old man Smitten's bier!"* And boys came dashing
out of the bushes, attaching themselves to the marchers, the Professor, who had suddenly regained his lost
youth, put himself at the vanguard and started singing, and Norman, who had been unable to repress his
bubbling musical exuberance, had got hold of his accordion again.

But as soon as they arrived at the farmhouse, the
women rushed forward, and when they saw their pastor in this unspeakable condition, they were filled
with compassion and pity for their unconscious shepherd. Despite objections from Carlsson, Mrs. Flod ran
inside to get a bedquilt to throw over him and cover
up the misery. Water was put on the stove to heat,
and clean linen and a suit of clothes were furnished
by the Professor. And when they reached the barn, the
sick man (as he was deferentially called, for nobody
wished to be so irreverent as to acknowledge that he
was inebriated) was laid to rest on a bed of dry straw.
Rundquist came with his cupping-glass and wanted to
bleed the Pastor but was shunted aside; and when he
couldn't have his way, he asked to be allowed at least
to say an incantation over the sick man, because he
knew a piece that would rid sheep of dropsy. But he
was told to stay away from the minister, just as the
rest of the men had been ordered to do.

Carlsson made his way stealthily to his attic room to
cleanse away all traces of his humiliation. When he
came inside and saw the enormity of the desecration in
the soiled bridal bed, he had a momentary sensation
of weakness, owing to fatigue brought on by the labor
of the last few days and nights. And he thought of
how different things would have been with Ida, if
their relationship had blossomed. He went over to the

* From "Songs of Fredman" (No. 27) by Karl Mikael Bellman
(1740–1795).—A.P.

window and gazed out over the cove with a long, sad look in his eyes. The clouds out there had scattered, and the mists had formed into white veils floating over the water; the sun was rising, and its rays—creeping into the bridal chamber—rested on Carlsson's pale face and on his watery eyes that were pinched together as though fighting back the tears. His hair fell in moist damp wisps down over his forehead, the white necktie was spotted and streaked with mud, and his wet coat sagged, hanging limply from his body.

The warmth of the sun seemed to give him a shivering chill, and running his hand over his brow he turned and again faced the desecration in the room.

"Oh, but this is real terrible!" he said, shaking himself out of his inertia. And with that he began pulling the bedclothes off the bed.

Chapter

6

CONDITIONS AND OPINIONS CHANGE.
FARMING FALLS OFF
AND MINING FLOURISHES.

Carlsson was not a man who allowed unpleasant impressions and sensations to affect him to a greater degree than he wished. He had stamina enough to take in his stride any storm that came along—be it hail or sleet or rain—to shake it off and forget about it. His position as farm proprietor he had gained through ability and know-how; and that the widow Flod had taken him as her lawful wedded husband was in his opinion as much to her advantage as to his own. However, after the intoxication of the wedding festivities had worn off, Carlsson began to show less enthusiasm for the farm chores, for he was now assured of his legal rights as the husband of old man Flod's widow and of his inheritance rights, since they were now expecting a child in a couple of months. His original notion of becoming a gentleman farmer he had given up, having come to realize that it could not be done; instead he had now decided to be content with being just an ordinary farmer, although one of some importance in the community. He went about in a fancy woolen jersey, wore a leather apron of no mean proportions, and paraded about in heavy sea boots. His favorite position was at the bureau with the desk-top, and there he spent a good deal of his time. He perused the newspapers, scribbled and figured less than before,

and oversaw the farm labor with pipe in his mouth,
but his interest in the farming was visibly diminishing.

"Farming is going down," he would remark, "that's
what the *noospapers* is saying; and it's cheaper nowadays to be *buying* your grain."

"You thought different before, Carlsson," Gusten
would comment. Gusten kept a close eye on everything that his stepfather said and did, and he subor-
dinated himself to him only out of apathy, in an in-
different sort of way, never accepting the role of son to
a man whom he still looked upon as an interloper.

"Times change, and so do we. I thank the Lord for
every day I get more sense in my head!" was Carlsson's
answer to Gusten.

And now he began to go to church regularly on
Sundays, took an interest in public affairs and was
elected a member of the community council. In this
manner he came in closer contact with Pastor Nordström and thus lived to see the memorable day when
he was permitted to address him in a more familiar
way—an ambition that Carlsson in his boundless
vanity had unceasingly harbored. And during the year
after that great event he never stopped alluding to
this social advancement whenever he engaged in conversation with the farm folk.

For the next year his conversation began and ended
with what the Pastor had said and what he, Carlsson,
had answered.

" 'But this time, my dear Nordström—this time you
must let me have my way,' I said to him, that's what I
said. And then Nordström says to me: 'Carlsson,' he
says, 'even though you are an intelligent man, and
sensible too,' he says, 'you mustn't be stiff-necked and
stubborn,' he says."

In the wake of these honors that had come to Carlsson, there followed others, and among these fire-
inspection was a favorite of his, for it consisted in his

traveling about the district at the expense of the county and of drinking coffee and brandy in the homes of people he knew. And despite the fact that the elections for parliamentary seats were held a good distance away on the mainland, they nevertheless brought with them corruption, temptations, and little reverberations that were felt away out in the skerries.

At election time and a couple of other times during the year, a baron in the district and his hunting companions would come to Hemsö in his steam yacht, and they would pay fifty crowns for the privilege of a few days of hunting. Then cognac and Swedish *punsch* flowed day and night; and when the hunting was over and the guests had departed, the general opinion prevailed that they were fine and generous folk.

As a result of all this, Carlsson kept coming up in the world and became a sort of shining light to the Hemsö folk: an authority endowed with a mental grasp of things which the rest of them were incapable of understanding. But there was one thing he was lacking in, one weak point that he had, and he was made aware of it from time to time: he was from the mainland and didn't know the first thing about the sea and the sea business.

In order to eradicate this last difference in social status, he began to stuff his brain full of nautical and fishing terms and showed an ever-increasing interest in the sea. He cleaned out a shotgun and went hunting, took part in seine-hauling and in the laying of herring-nets, and even had the courage to go on more distant sailing trips.

"Farming is going down and we have to get more out of the fishing," was his stock reply to his wife whenever she anxiously pointed out to him that the fields and cattle were falling into a state of neglect.

"The fishing comes first! Fishing's for the fisherman and farming's for the farmer!" was the gospel he now preached. After listening to the schoolmaster at the church council meetings and learning to phrase his words in *parlamentory* fashion, he could lay his words in a way that could not be resisted.

Whenever there were signs of diminishing returns from the farming, the farmhands were put to work chopping wood.

"The woods has to be thinned out so the trees can get room to grow! At least, that's what the *rationable* scientifical farmers is doing nowadays. I don't know myself—but that's what they're saying anyhow!"

And if Carlsson didn't know—how in the world would anybody else know?

Rundquist was now put in charge of the farming and Clara was to look after the cattle. Rundquist made the meadows into greenswards. After breakfast he would take a nap on the side of the ditch and doze until the noonday meal; after the noonday meal he napped in the bushes until it was time for supper. He also went back to his sorcery and cast a spell on the cows with the aid of a piece of steel when they gave no milk.

Gusten spent more time than ever out on the water, and he and Norman got together again on hunting expeditions. The momentary interest in farming which Carlsson had at one time spurred in them and which had made all hands labor diligently was gone; like Carlsson, they did not find it either enjoyable or rewarding to be working for someone else. And so life went on, idly and listlessly, but at the same time in a tranquil and placid manner.

In the early part of the fall—only a couple of months after the wedding—something happened to Carlsson's ship, which was only just setting out in full sail upon the Sea of Fortune. It was hit by a gale. His wife gave birth much too prematurely to a stillborn child. Her condition furthermore gave cause for anxiety, and the physician emphatically declared that she must never be with child again.

This was a fateful blow to Carlsson. After this event, his prospects were reduced sharply and all he had to look forward to were certain legal benefits. And as the wife's condition was worsened after the miscarriage, there was the dire threat that the change in his status might occur far sooner than anyone could have expected. And so he realized only too keenly that he would have to use the time that was left to full advantage, to strike up a partnership with iniquitous Mammon, to store away as much as he could lay his hands on, and concentrate on the days to come.

These thoughts stirred new life in Carlsson. The farming was to be given fresh impetus without delay; and if people asked for a reason, it was none of their concern. A new house was to be built in haste—and if anybody asked why, he didn't have to satisfy anyone's curiosity. And so timber was felled. Norman's mania for hunting had to be quenched immediately and he had once more to be enticed away from his friend Gusten; Rundquist, too, was captured and puffed up and shaken out of his lethargy by a promise of additional benefits and favors. All day long, the work of plowing, sowing, and fishing, as well as the carpentry on the new house, was in full swing, and Carlsson's communal activities were left in abeyance.

At the same time, Carlsson made himself into a homebody. He would sit at home with his old widow-wife and occasionally read a passage from Holy Writ or the hymnbook, addressing himself to the soft corner of her heart and appealing to her nobler feelings, although he was unable to make his meanderings understandable to the old woman, so that she could know exactly what was in his mind. The old woman liked having company and hearing someone talk, and she was grateful for these little attentions and took no noticeable account of what lay behind all this biblical education with its allusions to death—which passages Carlsson always chose to read.

One winter evening when the creek lay frozen, and

the bays and inlets and channels were unnavigable,
the Hemsö farm folk—who had been shut off from the
outside world and even from their closest neighbors
for fourteen days so that they could travel nowhere,
receive no visitors, not even a letter or a newspaper—
were gathered in the kitchen, Gusten among them.
The day had been short, for little work could be accomplished in the wintry weather; and the snow and
the loneliness had a depressing effect. A fire was burning on the hearth, and the two young men were at
work tying fishing-nets, the girls sat spinning, and
Rundquist was making spade handles. Heavy snow
had been falling all through the day and now reached
above the windowpanes so that the kitchen took on
the appearance of a room in which a corpse was to be
laid out. And every fifteen minutes one of the men
had to go outside and shovel away the snow from the
entrance so that they would not be snowed in and be
unable to get to the cattle-barn to milk the cows and
feed them for the night.

It was now Gusten's turn to go out and do the
shoveling, and with an oilskin coat over his jersey and
a sou'wester over his otter furcap, he prepared to go
outside. The snowdrifts were piled high against the
door. He pried it open and soon found himself standing on the slope in the wintry blizzard.

The air was murky; the snowflakes were as gray as
moths and the size of chicken feathers, and they kept
spinning down endlessly, ceaselessly, soundlessly pil-
ing one on top of another, first lightly and weight-
lessly until they had grown into a heap and had
become heavier and heavier, finally turning into a
compact mass that grew larger and larger. The snow
was already mounted high onto the sides of the farmhouse, and the glimmer of the light inside could only
be seen through the upper corners of the windowpanes.

Gusten then happened to see a streak of light com-

ing from the living room. He knew that his mother
and Carlsson were in there. Seized with a sudden
curiosity he cautiously pushed away some of the snow
on top until he had shaped a peephole. And when he
mounted the packed snow below he found he had a
view of the room. Carlsson was as usual seated at the
bureau-desk. In front of him he had a sizable document, which at the top bore the imprint of a large
blue seal that looked like the face of a banknote.
Carlsson was holding his pen as if on the point of
stabbing someone, and then Gusten saw that his
mother was standing beside the desk. The husband
seemed to be speaking for the wife as well as for himself and to be about to hand her the pen to sign her
name on the document.

Gusten put his ear to the pane, but all that he was
able to hear through the double storm windows was a
blurred mumbling. He was desperately anxious to
learn just what Carlsson was up to, for he had a suspicion that, whatever it was, it concerned him closely.
And he was aware of the fact that whenever anyone
put his signature to a printed document with a seal on
it, it was in connection with something of importance.

Slowly, softly, he opened the entrance door to the
hall, shed his straw shoes, crept upstairs and stood in
the attic hall. There he lay down on his belly, and
with head hanging down and ear cocked in the direction of the door to the living room, he was able to
distinguish what was being said in there.

"Anna Eva," he heard Carlsson preaching in a tone
betwixt and between that of an evangelist and a
member of a rural community council, "life is short
and death can come upon us before we know it.
Therefore it behooves us mortals to be prepared to
forsake this world; and it makes no difference *at all* if
this should come about today or tomorrow, for it's all
just the same! Therefore you may as well sign today as
tomorrow or any other day!"

The old woman did not like all this talk about death and the life hereafter, but Carlsson had for months talked about nothing else, so that by now she could only put up a lame resistance.

"Yes, but you see, Carlsson—it ain't the same to me if I die today or maybe ten years from now—and I can maybe live a long while yet."

"Ugh! I ain't saying you're *going* to die—all I say is that we *could* die; and it makes no difference if it should come about today or tomorrow or ten years from now, for it's got to come *some day* anyhow! Go ahead and write your name now!"

"Well—but I don't understand all this," said the wife, persistently struggling against signing, as if Death were already standing behind her with his scythe. "I don't see how it can . . ."

"Yes, but what difference does it make if it's got to be anyhow? And we don't none of us know for sure. Anyhow, *I*, for one, don't know! But go ahead and sign the paper anyhow!"

When Carlsson uttered his "Anyhow, *I*, for one, don't know!" the old woman might just as well have had a noose tightening round her neck for she was by that time completely bewildered, and she gave in.

"Well, but what's the idea of all this?" she inquired wearily, used up and exhausted by Carlsson's endless haranguing.

"Anna Eva, you must think of them what come after you—for that's the first and foremost duty of us human beings! And that's why I want you to put your name here!"

At that very moment Clara opened the kitchen door and asked where Gusten was. Gusten was not eager to be discovered lying on his belly and consequently did not make any reply; and after that interruption he could no longer follow what was being said in the living room.

Clara went back into the kitchen, and Gusten

scrambled down the stairs. He tarried outside the living-room door, and stood there listening; he heard Carlsson speak his final crucial, peremptory words, and he was then more than convinced that the document had been signed and his mother's will made. When he came back into the kitchen, the folk there noticed at once that something was the matter with him. He muttered under his breath about going to take a poke at a fox he had heard howling; about wishing he had gone to sea instead of staying at home and letting himself be eaten by lice; and he rambled about how a little bit of white arsenic powder mixed in with fodder could put new life into old nags and make them frisky—but that, if they were given too much, it could also be the end of them.

At the supper table, Carlsson was the perfect humanitarian. He inquired about Gusten's plans in the way of work and about his future hunting expeditions. Then he took the hourglass, and as the white sand ran down, he remarked ominously that "our few moments on this here earth of ours is very precious, so let's eat and drink, 'cause tomorrow we'll be dead! Skoal!"

That night Gusten lay awake into the wee hours. His head was filled with all kinds of sinister thoughts and diabolical schemes.

But Gusten was not a strong character, who could make conditions and circumstances conform to his own intentions and purposes, or who could translate thoughts into action. Once he had digested an idea and thought it out thoroughly, he abandoned it as though it had been completed and realized.

After a few brief hours of sleep, during which he dreamed about other matters, he was the usual, cheerful, easygoing Gusten again and for the moment forgot all about the incident, leaving it to the future and to justice to settle accounts with his stepfather.

Spring had come again, the swallows were busy mending their nests, and the Professor came back also.

During the past few years, Carlsson had laid out and started a garden. He had planted fruit trees and berry and lilac bushes, for which Pastor Nordström had given him branch-shoots and grafts, he had made sanded walks and paths, and built bowers and arbors. The farm was gradually beginning to take on the appearance of a regular gentleman's country estate. There was no denying that the intruder had brought both prosperity and comfort, not to say an attractive appearance, to the farm. He had put the cattle on their feet again, the land was in a state of hearty cultivation, and the farmhouse, barns, and other buildings, as well as the fences, were kept in good repair. He had even been able to raise the price paid for the fish and had arranged to have it forwarded by the steamboat to the fishmonger in the city; and in this way the tedious and time-consuming trips by sailboat were no longer necessary.

When Carlsson now began to grow lax and showed signs of being tired as he occupied himself with putting up the new house, the farm folk found fault and came with complaints.

"Why don't you try doing things on your own? Then you'll find out how easy it is!" was Carlsson's answer. "It's every man for himself, and God is with all of us!"

His new house was now finished, the roof had been laid, and he began to plant trees around it, made paths and walks, and kept digging and laying out flowerbeds.

He had built his little house with a certain display of taste so that it really put the two other houses on the farm to shame. It was small, had only two rooms and a kitchen on the lower floor, yet it had more distinction than the older dwellings. It was difficult to

say just why this was so—whether it was because he
had raised the roof-truss higher than is ordinarily
done and let the eaves extend a considerable distance
beyond the walls or because he had cut crosses in the
weatherboarding with a saw, or because he had added
a porch to the front of the house, with steps leading
up to it. There was nothing about the materials that
could be called costly, yet there was something villa-
like about the little house. It was ruddy as a cow but
the corners of the house-timbers were painted black
and were covered with weatherstripping, the boarded
window ledges were white, and the porch, covered by a
lightweight roof supported by four posts, was blue.

Carlsson had also shown his ingenuity in picking a
site at the very foot of a hill, an ideal location, which
was further enhanced by two ancient oak trees that
happened to be standing guard in front of the house,
almost as if they were the beginning of a contem-
plated tree-lined driveway or park. And seated on the
porch one had the most enchanting view: the cove
with its abundance of reed, the extensive green spring
field and the dip in the cow paddock, which provided
a vista of the inlet and cove with their sailboats in the
distance.

Gusten took a look at all this and went about
glowering. He would have liked nothing better than
to see all this undone; he glared and glowered at it as
he would have done at a wasp which was trying to
build a nest under a roof truss, a wasp that he would
have liked to rout out and destroy before it had had a
chance to lay its eggs and then, perhaps, together with
its offspring, remain as an uninvited guest. But, alas,
it was not in his power to put Carlsson out, and so the
stepfather sat where he was sitting.

The old woman was not in the best of health and
was satisfied that things were going well enough. She
had a notion that there would be strife and dissension
once she had gone the way of all mortals. But she did

not begrudge her husband a roof over his head so that he would not have to go around like a homeless beggar—for Carlsson was, after all, her lawfully wedded man. Her understanding of legal matters was very limited, but she had a vague feeling that the inventory of goods and chattels had not been conducted properly, neither was she satisfied with the way old man Flod's estate had been distributed and the manner in which her own will had been made. But these things could all be adjusted later; all she wanted now was to be free of such worries. And if things could not be settled now—before Gusten began to think about taking a wife—then they would surely be settled when that came to pass. And somebody must have put the idea of marriage into his head, for he was no longer his old self and went about lately looking as if somebody had put that lunatic notion into his head.

One afternoon at the end of May, Carlsson was standing in his new kitchen doing some masonry work around the stove, when Clara entered and yelled:

"Carlsson, Carlsson, the Professor has just come and he's brought a German gentleman with him what wants to see you!"

Carlsson was not slow in removing his leather apron. He wiped his hands and made himself ready to receive them, full of curiosity as to what could have brought about the rare visit.

When he had come out on the porch he bumped into the Professor and saw that he was accompanied by a stranger, who wore a long black beard and a shrewd expression on his face.

With a gesture in the direction of his companion, the Professor said as an introduction: "Diss iss Director Diethoff. He vishes to speak vith you, Carlsson."

Carlsson brushed off the bench on the porch and invited them to sit down.

Director Diethoff had not time to sit down, and, standing up, he took aim at Carlsson, asking him pointblank if he could buy Rågholmen.

Carlsson was almost knocked off his feet, wondering why in the world he would want to buy this rock in the sea, not much bigger than three acres in area, full of rocky knobs with only a scattering of spruce trees, and scarcely a patch of pasture where sheep could graze.

The director provided some information on that score. "For industrial purposes," he said laconically; and then he asked Carlsson's price.

The question bewildered Carlsson and he begged for time to think it over, so that he could meanwhile worm out what it might be that gave the little island its unexpected value. But to let Carlsson share this secret immediately did not enter into Director Diethoff's scheme; and so he recapitulated his question about the price of the islet and made a meaningful gesture toward his breast pocket, whose bulging appearance unmistakably pointed to the presence of an ample bundle of banknotes.

"Oh, I don't think it could be such a lot, I don't think," Carlsson said, "but I have to talk it over with the wife and son first."

Having said this, he lost no time in getting over to the farmhouse. He remained away for quite a while. When he returned, he looked nonplused and seemed to be hesitating as to what to say. Finally he managed to get out some words.

"Make me an offer! Tell me what you want to pay!" he shot out.

No, this proposition was not to Director Diethoff's liking.

"Well, then—if I say five—you wouldn't be thinking that's too much, would you?" Carlsson spluttered, all out of breath, the sweat running down his forehead in beads.

The German director opened his coat, took out his wallet and produced ten 100-crown banknotes.

"Here iss ein tousand paid in hand—on account.

Der four tousand dat remains, iss coming in der fall.
Ist das recht? Eh?"

Carlsson was not far from making a blunder but
pinched himself and stifled his overflowing feelings in
time. He succeeded in seeming moderately uncon-
cerned when he answered that the price was accept-
able. He did not let on that he had only meant five
hundred, although he had been given ten times that
amount. When the transaction was completed, they
all went down to the old woman and her son to put
the agreement in writing and to have her sign a
receipt for the advance payment. Carlsson blinked
and winked and grimaced to the two German bigwigs
to stand by him in his explanations to the mother and
the son, but they failed to grasp what he was grimacing for.

After signing the contract, the old woman put on
her eyeglasses and read the agreement.

She gave out a shriek. "Five thousand! What in all
the world . . . Why, you said five hundred, Carlsson!"

"Why, no! Oh, no, Anna Eva, you didn't hear right,
Anna Eva! Didn't I say five thousand, Gusten, didn't
I?" As he asked Gusten, he winked with his eyes so
flagrantly that the director could not help seeing it.

"Why, yes—that's what I thought—what I thought
you said—five thousand," Gusten said as a witness in
Carlsson's behalf and lying to the best of his ability.

When the document was signed and delivered,
Director Diethoff informed them that he would now
begin preparations for digging a feldspar mine on Rågholmen as a project of his company.

Nobody on Hemsö knew what feldspar was, and
nobody had ever imagined that there were any such
treasures out in the skerries. Naturally Carlsson was
an exception; he had, in fact, had thoughts in that
direction himself, but for lack of capital, he prevari-
cated, he had had to give up the idea.

The director thereupon explained that feldspar was

a kind of reddish mineral that was used in the manufacture of porcelain. Within a week or so, he said, the
overseer's house, which had already been ordered from
a construction firm, would be put up, and inside of
two weeks the wooden barracks for the workmen
would be installed. It would house thirty laborers,
and the mining operation would soon be in full
swing.

And having made this announcement, Director
Diethoff said goodbye and went away.

The golden shower had come upon them so unex-
pectedly, so suddenly, that Carlsson and the Hemsö
natives had not had time fully to realize and take into
consideration all its ramifications. They had one thousand in hand, four thousand more to come in the
fall—and all this for a rock in the water of no value to
them. This was much too much to have happened out
of a clear sky. And so they spent the whole evening
together in closest harmony, speculating about what
other advantages they might look forward to in the
way of added income and profit. There were, of
course, fish and farm products to be sold to the overseer and the many workmen; there was also firewood.
There could be no question about that. And then
there was the director himself—who perhaps would
bring his family with him to spend the summer, and
in that case they would certainly ask the Professor to
pay an increase in rent; and Carlsson might even have
an opportunity to rent his own house to someone,
and everything would be just fine.

Carlsson took charge of the money and locked the
ten banknotes in a compartment in the bureau-desk;
and half the night he sat up at the desk, making cal-
culations.

During the following week Carlsson made frequent
trips to Dalarö, bringing back with him carpenters
and painters and holding little receptions on the

veranda on his return. There he sat at a table, which he had placed there, drinking cognac and smoking a pipe, all the while supervising the work which was now progressing at a vigorous pace.

Soon wallpaper decorated the walls of the rooms, all the way out into the kitchen, where a Bolinder kitchen range was built in. The windows had green outside shutters, which created a bright effect, visible from far away; the porch was painted a different color —it now became white and rose—a blue-and-white striped awning was installed to provide shade on the side that was exposed to the sun; and gray latticework with white knobs enclosed the garden and the house.

The farmhands at Hemsö never tired of standing about gaping at the splendor—all but Gusten, who preferred to gaze at it from a distance, secreting himself behind some corner or a thick bush; and he rarely, if ever, accepted Carlsson's invitation to come to his porch.

It had been one of Carlsson's dreams, dreamed on nights when he lay fully awake and had a clear head, to be able to sit on a veranda the way the Professor did, self-indulgently leaning back in his chair and taking a sip now and then from a stemmed glass of cognac, gazing at the view and smoking a pipe. He would really have preferred smoking a cigar, but cigars were a little too strong for him.

As he sat like this on the veranda early one morning a week or so later, he heard a steamboat blowing its whistle in the inlet outside Rågholmen.

"They are here! They have come!" he thought; and as the lord and master of Hemsö he felt he ought to be polite and go and bid them welcome.

Consequently he went down to the farmhouse, dressed himself for the occasion and sent for Rundquist and Norman to ready themselves to go with him to Rågholmen and help receive the newcomers.

Half an hour later Carlsson's boat put out for the

little island, with himself at the tiller. Ever so often he
would tell them to row with measured strokes and to
keep time together, so that they would arrive like
decent, respectable folk.

When they had rounded the last rocky point and
the inlet widened, with Storön on one side and Rågholmen on the opposite, a splendid sight met their
eyes. In the cove lay a steam-yacht at anchor, decorated with pennants and signal-flags; and plying between the yacht and the shore were seen small jolly
boats with sailors in blue-and-white jerseys. High on
the rocky shore, which glimmered rosy-red from the
exposed feldspar veins, stood a group of gentlemen,
and a distance away could be seen a band of musi-
cians, whose brass instruments furnished a striking
picture, set as they were against the dark green of the
spruce trees.

The Hemsö oarsmen wondered what was going on
and what the strangers could be doing, and under
cover of the rocky coast they tried to row as close as
possible in order to be able to see and hear. No sooner
had they managed to come directly underneath the
spot where the gentlemen were assembled than a wind-
sweeping sound went through the air—as if a thousand or more eider ducks had winged aloft simultaneously. This was immediately followed by a roar that
seemed to emanate from within the mountain rock
itself, and a second later there was a crunching, burst-
ing noise as if the island had been rent asunder and
shattered into pieces.

"What the devil!" was all that Carlsson had time to
ejaculate, for almost in the same breath a torrent of
stones and rocks came swooping down upon them,
plunging into the water around the boat; and soon
after, sand and gravel rained down, and then came a
hailstorm of pebbles.

Not many minutes later, a voice was heard from the
top of the mountain. The speaker orated about indus-

trial progress, about arts and crafts, business and trade, about increased employment; and then something was said in a foreign tongue which the Hemsö natives were unable to understand.

Rundquist got the impression that it was a preacher who was speaking and took off his cap, but it was clear to Carlsson that it was none other than Director Diethoff who was doing the talking.

"Yes, chentlemen," said the director in his closing remarks, "we have before us a mass off stónes, und I conclute my speech vith de fervent hope that dese stones may all be turned into bread und sustenance!"

"Bravo!" shouted his audience.

With this, the band struck up a march. The gentlemen came marching down to the shore, keeping step with the music and carrying small pieces of rock, which they were turning over in their hands amidst laughter and jocular remarks to one another.

"What are you doing there in that boat?" shouted a gentleman in naval uniform to the Hemsö men, who were resting on the oars.

The men did not know what to answer; it never occurred to them that there might be any objection to their witnessing the ceremony.

"Why, I belieff it iss de lort und master off Hemsö himself! It iss Mister Carlsson, you know!" It was Director Diethoff who had stepped forward and was now enlightening his companions. He then presented Carlsson to them. "He iss our lantlort, you know! Now come und haff some breakfast with us!"

Carlsson could not believe his ears, but it was not long before he was convinced that it was no spurious invitation for he found himself seated at a table the like of which he had never seen before, set on the afterdeck of the yacht. At first he stood on ceremony, but the gentlemen were so very nice and friendly and didn't even want him to take off his leather apron. Rundquist and Norman, however, had to eat with the crew in the forecastle of the boat.

Even in his wildest imaginings Carlsson could not have thought of paradise as being more glorious. Here he saw a variety of food and delicacies the names of which he had never even heard of—food that melted in his mouth like honey—that burned in his throat like strong liquor—food of every color under the sun; and in front of him at his place, as at the plates of the other guests, there stood six glasses. And the different kinds of wines that were passed around made him think of the fragrance of blossoms, or the kiss of a pretty girl; wines that tickled and titillated his nostrils, made him tingle with excitement and stirred him to laughter. And all through this delightful repast, the band played the loveliest music so entrancingly that he felt a moist throbbing at the root of his nose. One moment he was on the point of giving way to tears, the next he felt a chill at his temples, and at intervals his body experienced the most exhilarating and intoxicating sensation from head to foot so that he could have died happy at that moment.

When the repast was over, Director Diethoff paid tribute to the company's Hemsö landlord in a speech. He praised him for being an honor to his calling in life and for not having abandoned the basic source of livelihood for uncertain profit in other pursuits or occupations, where poverty walked hand in hand with luxury. And after that, they all drank a toast to him. Carlsson didn't know when to laugh or when to appear serious, for he saw the gentlemen burst into laughter when things were said which he thought were of an exceedingly serious nature—and so he did as the others did, and laughed, too.

When the company had left the table, coffee and cigars were passed around. Carlsson, now in seventh heaven and generously oozing good cheer, was stalking toward the bow to make sure that the two men had been properly taken care of, when the director called to him and asked him to step into his cabin for a moment.

When they had come inside, Director Diethoff made the proposal that Carlsson—to consolidate his position and in order to be able to wield greater authority over the workmen on the island if intercession should be warranted—invest in a few shares in the syndicate.

"Well, now—that's something I don't know nothing about," said Carlsson, who wasn't entirely innocent when it came to business deals; for he had learned that one should never close a transaction after having had a few drinks.

But the director would not let go of his victim, and after a half hour Carlsson was the owner of forty shares at one hundred crowns each in the Eagle Feldspar Corporation; and he was, besides, given the promise that he would be elected special auditor. Carlsson promptly asked the director to write down the title for him on a sheet of paper. Nothing was said about payment for the shares—that could be taken care of little by little—in installments.

After this there was still more coffee and cognac and *punsch,* and then mineral water was served; and it was six o'clock before Carlsson was ready to get into his boat and sail home.

When he disembarked from the yacht, the sailors manned the gangway, lining up on each side. This honor was something Carlsson was in total ignorance of and so he grabbed each sailor's hand and shook it, and invited each and every one of them to drop in and see him when they were at Hemsö.

And holding on to his forty shares of stock with their attached coupons, he was rowed home in style, sitting nonchalantly at the tiller, with a Regalia cigar between his jaws and a basket of Swedish *punsch* between his knees.

When he arrived home, Carlsson was in a state of bliss. He went from one end of the house to the other, treating everyone to *punsch,* even the kitchen help, and displaying the stock certificates, which looked like blown-up government banknotes. He wanted to invite the Professor, but when the others demurred, he replied to their objections by stating that he was quite as good as any German musician for he was now a special auditor; besides, the Professor was not a man of learning, and therefore he was not a *real* professor. Carlsson now had grandiloquent plans for the future. He was going to form a combine, consolidating all the salting of herring done in the skerries, and bring coopers from England, and charter freighters to carry cargoes of salt direct from Spain. At the same time he spoke of basic resources and of those who pursued farming and made their livelihood by it; he described what the future held for it, expressed his apprehension and fears, and also his hopes. All kept downing his *punsch* and enveloped themselves in clouds of tobacco smoke and cheerful illusions about Hemsö's glorious future.

Carlsson had climbed to the top of his rock of ambition and began to feel dizzy. The tilling of the soil—the basic source of sustenance and production—was relegated to a backseat, and visits to Rågholmen became a daily habit. He struck up an acquaintance with the mining overseer and sat on his porch, drinking cognac and Biliner water,* watching the workmen breaking up rocks to get at the crystalline veins, an operation that delayed and was an obstacle to transporting the entire mass of rocks in one or two shiploads.

The overseer was an oldtimer who had been the boss of a mining camp. He was sensible enough to truckle to the shareholder and special auditor, and he had sufficient insight into the mining business to be able to judge how long the mining would last.

The mining operation on Rågholmen, however,

* A mineral water from the Biliner Sauerbrunnen in Germany.—A.P.

had its particular influence on the physical and moral wellbeing of the Hemsö folk, and the presence of thirty unmarried workmen soon began to have its effect.

The customary tranquillity was interrupted. All day long, blasting and rumblings were heard from the rocky little island; steamboat whistles sounded from the inlet and the cove; yachts arrived, tying up at Hemsö and spewing flocks of seamen ashore. In the evenings, the mine workers would come to the farm and hang around the well and the barn, trying to waylay the girls; they got together and organized dances, had drinks with the young men and the boys, and ever so often started fights. The people at the farm guzzled most of the night, and so they were neither in a mood nor in a condition for work during the day; they slept when they were out in the fields, and those who had their work in the kitchen stood nodding over the stove. Now and then the overseer would come to Hemsö for a visit, and then the coffee-pot was put on. And as a fine gentleman like that could not be offered mere ordinary liquor, there had always to be cognac on hand. But the Hemsö farmers did a brisk business selling fish and butter, and money streamed in so that they could live well and eat plenty; and meat was now seen on the table more often than before.

Carlsson was beginning to get fat and constantly showed the effects of the previous night's drinking. However, he was never excessively drunk, and to him the summer passed like one long ecstasy in which he divided his time between mining, communal tasks and prettifying his own little house.

He had been away on a fire inspection tour for about a week in the early fall, and when he came back home early one morning his wife met him with the alarming news that something must have happened out at Rågholmen. Not a sound had been heard from there in the past four days; not a single blast had been set off, and they had heard no steamboat whistles. The folk at Hemsö had been occupied with the threshing and therefore unable to row over to the island. And no one had seen anything of the overseer either, and the workmen had ceased lazying around at Hemsö in the evenings. This could only mean that something was wrong, and in order to satisfy his curiosity, Carlsson harnessed up his yokefellows, which was what he called Rundquist and Norman whenever he wanted them to row him out to the mining installations. He had had the rowboat painted white with a border of blue at the railing; and to stress his importance as a farm proprietor and to look more impressive where he sat at the tiller, he had made a pulley with the aid of old curtain cord. By means of this contraption he could sit up straight as an arrow and do the steering. And in order further to impress onlookers when they saw him coming, he had instructed Rundquist and Norman minutely in the essence of oarsmanship.

The rowing was done briskly for they were spurred on both by curiosity and anxiety; and when they arrived at Rågholmen, they were astonished to see the desolation that lay over it.

It was as silent there as in a grave, and not a human being could be seen. They went ashore and climbed over rock fragments and shattered stones. The overseer's house was gone, and all the tools and implements had disappeared; nothing but the barracks, as the laborers' shanty was called, had been left behind, but now it was deserted and showed signs of vandalism; everything in the way of furnishings and what was not fastened down had been removed: doors, windows, benches, and bunks.

"By God, it looks as if they skipped for good!" Rundquist evaluated the situation.

"So it does," Carlsson concurred and promptly harnessed up again, this time setting off for Dalarö, where he figured there must be mail for him at the post office.

He had guessed right, for there he found a voluminous letter from Director Diethoff announcing the dissolution of the corporation and the cessation of its mining operation, owing to the unsatisfactory quality of the raw material. And since Carlsson's claim for four thousand crowns against the corporation was balanced by the forty shares he had acquired but not yet paid for, there remained no outstanding business between the corporation and the above-mentioned Carlsson and associates.

"Swindled out of four thousand," Carlsson thought to himself. "Well, I'm glad it wasn't no more!"

And with the bird-of-passage nature that was his, despite the fact that he hailed from the mainland, he shook his feathers and was again just as dry as before; and when he read what the director had written in a postscript—that whatever the company had left behind on Rågholmen became the property of Hemsö, if the folk there should care to remove it—he felt even drier.

Carlsson was a trifle downcast when he came home after this outing. He had lost a considerable amount of money, and also his fancy title. Gusten showed a temptation to rub salt into the wound, but Carlsson magnanimously dismissed the whole matter with a gesture.

"Pshaw! It ain't worth talking about! It ain't worth talking about at all!"

But the next day he and his three farmhands were in full activity on Rågholmen, bringing back boards and bricks and building material in the big flat-bottomed boat. And before long he had built himself a little summer cabin of one room and a kitchen down by the creek. And he built it in a spot which no one had ever thought of, where he had a view of not only the cove but the whole surrounding landscape.

The summer was over, and with it its buoyant, lighthearted dreams. Winter was approaching, and the atmosphere grew dense and oppressive, dreams and aspirations took on a darker hue, and reality had a different aspect; for some it was brighter, for others there were threatening clouds on the horizon.

Chapter

7

CARLSSON'S DREAMS COME TRUE.
THE BUREAU-DESK IS UNDER
CLOSE SURVEILLANCE BUT THE
SELF-APPOINTED PUBLIC ADMINISTRATOR
TAKES CHARGE AND LOCKS AND SEALS IT.

Although Carlsson had been married only a few brief
years, his marriage had not been what is commonly
called a happy one. His better half was well along in
years, although not old enough to be a burden, and
Carlsson himself was approaching the dangerous age.
Up to the time he was forty, his life had been one of
drudgery. He had always had to work hard to earn his
bread and butter and to make ends meet; and the girl
he had wanted most to marry had refused him. Now
that he had achieved his ambitions and could look
forward to an old age of peace and quiet, the flesh
began to make itself felt, perhaps more insistently
than usual because the farm chores had been less
strenuous during the past year, and possibly also because he had been suppressing his carnal desires until
the flesh rebelled. As he sat relaxing in the pleasant
warmth of the kitchen, his mind, willingly or unwill-
ingly, began to play tricks on him, and his eyes got
into the habit of pursuing Clara's young body as she
went in and out of the living room. With time his
glances would linger on her figure, would make them-

selves at home and tarry there, only to take little
jaunts and excursions here and there and then fly
away and come back again. It was not long before the
girl sat fixed before his eyes; and no matter where he
went, he could not get rid of her. However, there was
someone else who was looking also—although not at
Clara but at the eyes that kept following and pursuing
her. And the more this person watched, the more her
imagination was stirred up, until it became like a
growth embedded in her own eye, and it ached and
throbbed and grew into a festering sore.

It was several days before Christmas Eve. Darkness
had set in, but the moon had risen and cast its lumi-
nous beams upon the snow-bedecked spruce trees, over
the mirrorlike cove, and upon the white-carpeted
ground. A biting, searching north wind was pushing
forward, sweeping the dry snow ahead of it. Clara was
standing in the kitchen, heating up the bake-oven
while Lotten was busy kneading the dough.

Carlsson had taken a seat over by the cupboard in
the corner. He was smoking his pipe and was purring
like a cat in the warmth of the kitchen. His eyes
played hither and thither and rambled about in the
blazing heat, wallowed in lust and stared passionately
when they fell upon Clara's white, bare arms, protruding from her linen waist.

"Ain't you going to do the milking first before we
sweep and clean up?" Lotten asked Clara.

"That's what I mean to do," Clara replied, putting
on a sheepskin jacket after putting away the fire rake
and the straw broom. Then she lighted the barn
lantern and went outside, and a moment later Carlsson got up and followed her.

Not long after, the old woman entered from the
living room and asked where Carlsson was.

"He went to the barn—right after Clara left," was
Lotten's answer.

Without asking any further questions, Carlsson's wife took a lantern and lit it, and then she, too, went out.

The wind was sharp and bitter, yet she refused to go back and put on something to keep her warm, for it was only a stone's throw to the barn. It was slippery on the rocky path, and the snow was blowing about her like flour-dust, but she made her way to the barn at a fairly brisk pace. She hastened inside and went straight into the cowhouse where it was warm. There she found a place where she could listen, and heard whispering coming from the sheepfold. In the dim moonlight, which filtered through the cobwebs and the chaff of hay that covered the windowpanes, she could see the cows turning their heads and gazing at her with wide-open eyes that glistened green in the darkness. She saw the milking-stool standing there, and also the milking-pail—but it was not this she had come to see—it was something else—something she would give anything *not* to see—something that compelled her, like the sight of a man being beheaded—and, at the same time, almost frightened her to death.

She skipped across the straw-littered floor through the cowhouse, and came into the sheepfold. It was dark in there, and no sound was heard; the light in the lantern had been put out, but the tallow candle in it was still smoking. The sheep moved about uneasily and kept tugging and nibbling at some branches with withered leaves. No—no, it was not this she was driven to witness—and so she kept going and came into the henhouse. There she found the hens sitting on their perches, clucking and chucking among themselves as though they had just been awakened from their sleep.

The door, opening outwardly, stood ajar, and now she was out in the moonlight again. Two pair of shoes —a small foot and a large one—had left their tracks

in the snow—tracks that seemed blue in the shadows;
and they led toward the heavegate to the paddock,
and she saw that it had been raised. She kept on going
as though hooked onto someone who was dragging her
on and on; and all along the snowy ground the tracks
were visible as if they had been left by the chain to
which she was riveted, and which was being hauled in
from some blind, hidden spot inside the paddock.

It was an overpowering, goading feeling that drove
her forward irresistibly into the very same paddock,
past the same heavegate, under the same hazel bushes
where once before, at another junction in her life—a
grim, harassing, awesome moment—she had lived
through a night that she had wished never to be reminded of. But this time the hazel bushes stood de-
nuded, showing only the beginning of sprouting buds
that looked like tiny cabbage worms; and the oak
trees, though still standing there, their hard, tough,
brown leaves rustling in the wind, were now so
thinned out that the dark-green sky was visible
through them.

The path that the chain took became longer and
longer. It snaked its way in among the spruce trees
and under them, and the trees shook off some of the
snow from their overburdened boughs on her sparse,
graying hair as she stumbled against them; the snow
came crashing down over her striped woolen jumper,
blew down her back and neck, and made her feel cold
and wet through and through.

She plunged farther and farther into the wood
where woodgrouse were roused from their nightly
slumber and flew up from their perches, startling and
frightening her; she went across the shaky, treacherous
swamps and marshes which quaked and tottered with
every step she took, and over old wooden fences which
creaked as she struggled across them.

The tracks were the same: two pair of feet, side by
side, one small foot, the other a larger one; sometimes

they stepped into each other's tracks, and sometimes they stepped around each other, as if they had been dancing along; they went across fields filled with stumps and stubble, where the wind had cleared away the snow; over stoneheaps, ditches, piled-up stakes for fencing, and over wind-fallen trees.

She had not the slightest idea how long she had been tramping but her hands felt numb and her head frozen, and she blew repeatedly on her thin, red hands and then tucked them inside her skirt. She wanted to turn back and go home the same way she had come, but it was too late to be thinking of that now; and the way back might be no shorter than continuing straight ahead. And so she kept going through a grove of aspen whose surviving leaves trembled and quivered as if frozen by the icy north wind; and at long last she came to a stile over a fence.

The moonbeams lighted the spot clearly and sharply, and she could plainly see that they had been sitting there. She could see the impression of Clara's skirt, of her jacket with the sheepskin trimming. So this was where it had happened! Here! Her knees began to tremble; a chill went through her as though her blood had frozen in her veins; yet all the while it burned within her as if her blood had turned into boiling water.

She felt as if all her strength had left her and she had to sit down on the stile to rest. She cried hysterically, gave out scream after scream, and then all of a sudden she quieted down, got up, and climbed over the stile.

From the other side of the fence she could see the creek. It lay black, shining in the moonlight like a mirror, and just beyond she could see the lights from the little farmhouse, and another light in the barn. The wind still blew with a cutting bite, chilling her whole body and tearing at her thin, wispy hair; her nostrils felt like ice. Half running, she reached the creek and stood upon the frozen water, glided forward on the shaky, undulating surface, and heard the sound of the withered reeds rustling about her ears and snapping under her feet which suddenly hit against a buoy that lay frozen in the ice. She fell headlong on the icy surface but got up again and started running as if Death were pursuing her and burning her flesh with a branding iron. She was within a few steps of the opposite shore when her foot crashed through the ice, which had been pitched back by the ebbing water and deposited on the slimy, muddy bottom like a windowpane and which broke under her weight with a tinkling, crunching sound. She felt the cold increasingly numbing her legs but dared not cry out for fear that someone would come down and ask her where she had been. Coughing as if her lungs were about to burst, she dragged herself out of the slimy icehole, stole up the sloping hillock, went straight to her bed in the living room, lay down on it, and asked Lotten to start a fire in the stove and make some elderflower tea; and she kept to her bed and did not get up.

The girls took off her wet clothes, covered her with quilts and sheepskin and woolfell, and made a brisk fire of long wooden logs; yet she kept shaking and freezing, and her teeth chattered. Then she asked the girls to fetch Gusten, who was in the kitchen, and he came in.

"Are you sick, Mother?" he asked in his usual placid manner.

"This is the last of me," was the old woman's answer. She was gasping for breath. "I ain't never going to get up again. . . . Shut the door and open the desk in the chiffonier there—they key is behind the horn with the gunpowder in it—you know where it is, Gusten. . . ."

Gusten became depressed and did as he was told.

"Open the lid—pull out the third drawer to the left—and take out the large envelope what you see there—yes, that's it! —Now throw it into the fire!"

Gusten put the bulky envelope into the fire, and it

blazed and burst into flames, the paper curled up, charred, and then turned black as coal.

"Close the door, my boy, and lock the bureau-desk! Put the key in your pocket! Then sit down by the bed here and listen careful to what I say, Gusten, for to-morrow I ain't going to be able to speak no more!"

Gusten sat down beside her. He shed a few tears, for he now began to understand that his mother was really in earnest.

"When I've closed my eyes—I want you to take your father's seal—and you have it already—and then I want you to seal up every blessed keyhole in the cabinet until the public administrator and his men come to the house here. . . ."

"And what about Carlsson?" Gusten asked, wavering.

"Let him have his own house—I don't know that anybody can take that away from him—but that's all he gets—and if you can buy back his rights to it, then do it! May God bless you and take good care of you, Gusten—it's too bad you couldn't have got to the wedding in time, Gusten—but I guess you had your good reason for staying away. . . . And now let me tell you—you must promise to be sensible. . . . When I'm gone, I don't want no fancy coffin with silver plate trimmings . . . one of them with yellow stain on—the kind what you see in the city at Slussplan is good enough—and I don't like a whole lot of folk standing 'round me neither—but bells I want—and if the Pastor would like to say a word or two, let him—and you can give him your father's meerscum pipe with the silver lid on it and a side of mutton for Mrs. Nordström—and then, Gusten, you got to see about getting married—and you should take a girl what you are sure you like—and stick to her—but be sure you get a girl of your own kind—and if she's got money, don't let that stand in the way—but don't take no girl what ain't so good as yourself—for all they do is to eat you up like lice—and remember, 'birds of a feather'—well, you know the rest. . . . Now I like you to read a few words of comfort to me—then I'll try to get some sleep. . . ."

Just then the door opened and Carlsson slithered in, meek but full of confidence.

"If you are sick, Anna Eva," he said in a matter-of-fact voice, "we'll get the doctor for you."

"Don't bother!" answered the old woman, turning her back to him. Carlsson began to suspect that she was aware of what had happened and tried to pacify her.

"You ain't mad with me, Anna Eva? Pshaw, you ain't going to be mad with me for that? That ain't nothing to get mad for! —You want me to read something to you from the Book, eh?"

"Don't bother!" was her only answer.

Carlsson realized now that there was nothing for him to do, and since he was averse to any unnecessary effort, he accepted the situation as it was and sat down on the sofa with the railback, to see what would happen. As everything had been settled to his advantage, and the old woman had neither the interest nor the strength to enter into conversation with him, there was nothing that could be added. And as for matters concerning him and Gusten—why, they could be adjusted later, no doubt about that.

No one gave a second thought to getting a doctor; people out on Hemsö were used to dying without one —besides, all communication with the mainland had been interrupted, owing to the snowfall and weather conditions.

For two days and two nights Gusten and Carlsson kept watch over the sickroom and each other. When one of them fell asleep on his chair or on the sofa, the other snoozed with one eye open. But whenever one of them stirred or moved an eyelid, the other one would give a start.

On the morning before Christmas old Mrs. Carlsson lay dead in her bed.

For Gusten it was as if only in that moment the umbilical cord had been severed; as though he had only then been cut loose from his mother's womb and suddenly changed into an independent human being.

After closing his mother's eyes and placing a hymn-book under her chin to keep her mouth from sagging, he lighted a candle, took out the sealing wax and his father's seal, and put the bureau-desk under lock and seal before Carlsson's very eyes.

The passionate hatred the two men had for each other, and which they had suppressed for so long, now came to the surface. Carlsson rose and placed himself in front of the bureau-desk, turned his back to it, and faced Gusten.

"Just a minute! What do you think you're doing, boy!" he spluttered.

"I ain't no boy no more!" Gusten replied in no uncertain tone. "This is my farm—and I'm the master of Hemsö now—and you don't belong in this house no more!"

"Is that so? You'll soon find out about that!" Carlsson bullied.

Gusten went over to the wall and took down a shotgun hanging there. He cocked the trigger so that the cartridge was clearly visible to Carlsson, tapped the barrel with his fingers, and—for the first time in his life—he roared:

"Get out! Get out! Or I'll let you have it!"

"Are you threatening me?"

"That's just what I'm doing! And you ain't got no witnesses neither!" Gusten answered in a tone so steady that it sounded as if he had been consorting with lawyers of late.

This was plain, straightforward talk, and Carlsson could not fail to understand it.

"You wait! You just wait until you hear the will read!" he said and went out into the kitchen.

With a corpse in the house and with no possibility of getting to town for either shroud or coffin, Christmas Eve at Hemsö was a drab and dreary one that year. The snow came down unceasingly, making it dangerous to cross creeks and coves either by foot or by boat. To put a boat into the water was unthinkable, for the water was one mass of sludge and slush and broken-up pieces of ice through which one could neither row nor sledge, much less travel on foot.

Carlsson and Flod—as Gusten preferred to be called now—passed each other, and sat down at table together, but never spoke. Everything in the house was in disorder, nobody had the initiative to get anything done, and everyone looked to someone else to do the work, so that most of the household duties were left undone.

Christmas Day came with troubled sky, gray and misty, and snow was falling again. To think of getting to church was as much out of the question as going anywhere else; and so as the next best thing Carlsson read aloud a makeshift sermon in the kitchen.

Having a death in the house put out of mind all Christmas festivity. The meals were carelessly prepared, nothing was ready on time, and everyone was discontented and in bad humor. There was something oppressive in the air, both within the house and outside; and since the old woman lay dead in the living room, they all had to spend their time in the kitchen. It was like being confined to quarters somewhere; and when they were not eating or drinking, they slept— one on a sofa, another on a bed. Playing a game of cards or a tune on the accordion was something they deferentially abstained from.

The day after Christmas Day came and went, and the dull atmosphere of gloom and depression remained. But by this time Gusten Flod had begun to lose patience. He realized that any further postpone-ment in removing the corpse could have serious con-sequences since it was beginning to decompose, and so he took Rundquist with him to the carpentry shed and there they joined together a coffin which they stained yellow. And after that was done, Gusten's mother was wrapped in a winding-sheet sewn together from odds and ends found in the house. Then the fifth day set in; and because there was still no sign that the weather would be changing for the better, it seemed that they might have to wait a couple of weeks before Mrs. Carlsson's body could be brought to the church and buried in her grave. And so it was decided to try to get her there by whatever means they could. To carry out their intention, they put the big, flat-bottomed boat into the water, and all the men got ready for a run through the ice with the help of sledges, icehooks, axes, and ropes. And early in the morning of the sixth day, they started off on their dangerous sea voyage. Occasionally, when they found a stretch of water which had been kept free of ice by the current, they took to the oars and rowed. But when they came into a cove which was frozen solid, they had the hard work of getting the boat up onto the sledges. And when they had contrived to do that, all hands had to summon fresh energy to move the boat ahead. The worst places were those where sludge and slush and broken-up ice had gathered in masses; there the oars merely plashed up and down, and the boat would not move ahead more than a few inches at a time. Here and there it was deemed best to hew a channel in the ice with hooks and axes. But heaven help him who made a misstep and swung his ax with too much force and got beyond the end of the channel where the current had eaten away and weakened the ice, leaving only a treacherously thin crust!

A good part of the day had passed and it was afternoon before they took the time either to eat or drink anything—and they had still another cove to traverse. As far as the eye could see, one enormous field of snow lay stretched ahead of them, dotted with roundish elevations here and there, miniature rocks, covered with snow. In the east the sky was a bluish black, signifying that more snow could be expected; the crows flew in from the outer skerries, winging their way inland to seek refuge for the night; occasionally a roaring, rumbling sound would be heard from the ice, as though it were about to thaw; and from out in the open sea came the sound of barking seals. The eastern side of the cove merged with the open sea, but no breaks in the ice could be detected out there. Yet they thought it strange when they suddenly imagined they heard a long-tailed duck somewhere in the direction of the outer skerries. But as they had had no communication with the mainland for the past two weeks, they could not know whether the lighthouses were functioning or not. However, they took it for granted that they would be extinguished during the Christmas holidays and until the New Year.

"This is as far as we'll be getting!" Carlsson declared after having been silent most of the time.

"We'll be getting there! We *got* to get there!" answered Flod, at the same time putting his shoulder to the sledge. "But we got to put in at Måskläppan and get us something to eat first."

And so they set their course for a rocky island lying in the middle of the cove, pulling the boat behind them on the sledge.

The island, however, lay farther away than it seemed; and the closer they came to it, the less they recognized it as Måskläppan. Finally they were within cablelength.

"Icehole ahead!" shouted Norman, who was the lookout. "Keep to the left!"

The sledges swung to the left, then a little more to

the left, and finally they had circled the rock. It seemed to be out of reach from all sides, in any case by sledge, for the hot rays of the sun—before the misty gray set in—or perhaps a warm undercurrent, had melted the ice close to the rock so that a channel had been formed around the islet, isolating it from the surrounding mass of ice. Twilight was now falling, and something had to be done quickly. Young Flod, who had assumed full command of the operation, proposed the plan of attack. The boat was to be slipped off the sledges onto the icy surface and then pushed along the ice until they came to the open channel; at that very moment everyone was to jump aboard and put out the oars.

"One-two-three," commanded Flod, and the boat gathered momentum, but the forward sledge gave way, the boat capsized, and the coffin fell into the sea.

Frightened out of their wits by the dreadful happening, Flod and Carlsson—both of whom had been pushing from the stern—forgot to jump aboard and were left behind, standing at the edge of the ice field. Rundquist and Norman, however, got onto the boat safely.

Having been hammered together hurriedly, the coffin box was leaky, and soon filled with water and sank to the bottom before any of the men could gather their wits sufficiently to think of anything but themselves.

"We got to get to the church this minute!" Flod ordered. Gusten Flod showed more energy on this day than good common sense.

Carlsson was quick to object, but when Gusten asked him if he would relish the idea of standing on the edge of the ice all night, he demurred no longer, for he now realized that it would be impossible to reach the rocky islet.

Rundquist and Norman had in the meantime succeeded in clambering ashore and were shouting and

beckoning to their two comrades to join them. But
Flod's only answer was to wave his hand in a goodbye
as he pointed toward the southern end of the cove
where the church and the parsonage stood.

Carlsson and Gusten trudged on for some time and
neither one of them spoke a word. Gusten marched
ahead with the icehook to test whether the ice was
solid enough for them to walk on. Carlsson, his coat-
collar turned up, followed in his steps, gloomy and
dejected after his wife's sudden and gruesome end in
the deep of the sea.

When they had been tramping along for half an
hour or so, Gusten halted to catch his breath and then
looked about, his eye wandering from rock to rock
and from shore to shore, trying to determine just
where they were.

"Well, I'll be damned! I think we've taken the
wrong direction!" he growled. "That rock there ain't
Måskläppan, for Måskläppan is over there!" he said,
pointing to the east. "And you see that lone pine tree
on that isle there? That's Gillöga!"

With this he gestured in the direction of a low,
elongated island not far from the coastline, pointing
out a pine tree which had been left to itself up on a
height, where the rest of the trees had been cleared.
With its two remaining boughs—and resembling a
sort of signal apparatus—it was now a well-known
land-and-sea-mark.

"And over there's Trälskär!"* Gusten exclaimed.
He was talking to himself and shaking his head.

Carlsson was getting worried, for the skerries were
still a closed book to him, and he had had unlimited
confidence in Gusten's familiarity with them.

Gusten Flod had apparently come to realize the situation he was in; he changed his course and set off in
a more southerly direction.

Dusk had now set in, but the snow lighted their

* The correct name is Trätskär.—A.P.

path a little so that they could still sight land. They exchanged no words, but Carlsson followed close in the tracks of his leader.

All of a sudden Flod stopped and cocked his ear. Carlsson—not being trained to the sounds of the skerry wasteland—could hear nothing, but Flod seemed to be apprehensive about a faint roar in the distance, coming from the east, where clouds had appeared and formed into a regular wall, thicker and darker than the misty veil which enveloped the horizon.

For a moment they stood still. Then Carlsson, too, was able to hear a low, ominous roaring and booming sound, coming nearer and nearer.

"What is that?" he asked with a quiver, moving closer to Gusten.

"It's the sea!" Gusten replied. "Within half an hour we'll be swept off our feet by a whirling snowstorm! And if the wind is real bad it'll break up the ice! Then God only knows what'll happen to us! We have to move fast!"

He hastened along on the ice as fast as he dared, and Carlsson followed after him. The snow was spinning in flurries around their feet, and the roaring, ominous sound seemed to be trying to catch up with them.

"This is the end of us!" Gusten suddenly cried. He stopped for a brief second and pointed to a light flashing from behind a rock to the southeast. "The beacon is lit—that means that the ice has broken up and the water is clear!"

Carlsson was still only vaguely conscious of the impending danger, but when he saw that Gusten was frightened, he began to realize that something perilous was in the offing.

By this time the easterly wind had caught up with them, and they could see the onrushing wall of snow only a stone's throw away, moving toward them like

an enveloping screen of pillars; the next moment the
snow was whirling about them, falling in dense, heavy
clouds, and black as smoke. They were surrounded by
total darkness, and the pale, blurred light flickering
from the lighthouse suddenly went out, after having—
like an auxiliary sun—helped them to find their way
for a few brief minutes.

Gusten continued trotting along at a brisk pace,
and Carlsson trod as close on his heels as he was able
to; but he had his weight to contend with and could
not keep up; he grew short of breath, and begged
Gusten to slacken off. But Gusten had no desire to
die, and so he continued running—running for his
life! Carlsson caught up with him and tugged at the
tail of his coat, imploring him over and over again not
to leave him behind, promising him anything he
wished for; and when this did not help, he cursed and
swore and condemned him to the cesspool of hell—
but all to no avail.

"Every man for himself, and God be with us all!"
Gusten answered back; and he cautioned Carlsson to
stay a few paces behind—for the ice might otherwise
crack and give way.

It seemed, as a matter of fact, to be beginning to
weaken already, and the crackling, cracking sounds of
ice breaking up behind them grew louder and more
frequent. What was worse, the roaring sea was now
approaching so unmistakably that they could hear the
surging waves breaking and thumping against the
rocks and the edge of the ice field, exciting seagulls
and mews that now began screeching, looking forward
to fresh, unexpected prey.

Carlsson was now out of breath, panting and
puffing. The distance between Gusten and him grew
longer, and finally he found himself running all by
himself in the darkness. Occasionally he stopped short,
searching for Gusten's tracks, but they had been ob-

literated almost immediately by the swirling snow. He shouted, but no answer came back. He was alone— alone in the murky night with the frosty, freezing cold and the icy sea—and with death. . . .

Egged on by terror, he started running again. He ran so fast that he saw the snowflakes spinning backward even though they flew in the same direction in which he was going. And then he cried out again, cried at the top of his voice.

"Keep going with the wind, and you'll come west! You'll find land there!" he heard a fugitive voice coming fitfully through space from the darkness ahead. And after that there was silence again.

By this time Carlsson had no strength left. He could run no longer. His courage was gone. He continued forward, step by step, at a considerably slackened pace, no longer able to fight back; and all the while he heard the turbulent sea rolling in behind him, roaring, surging, heaving, and groaning, as if it were out in search of prey on this awesome night.

Pastor Nordström had gone to bed at eight in the evening and had been reading the diocesan newspaper. After reading for a while, he had fallen asleep and now lay in a sound slumber. But around eleven that night he felt his wife nudging him with her elbow and heard her calling to him.

"Erik! Erik!" he heard her say in his sleep.

"What's the matter with you? Can't you be still? Compose yourself!" he growled, not yet awake.

"Compose myself? I am as calm as can be!"

Afraid that he might have to listen to a long-winded harangue in explanation, the Pastor hastened to reassure his better half that he was convinced she did not mean to disturb him, and lighting a match, asked what was the matter.

"There is someone down in the garden—someone who is calling to you! Can't you hear?"

The Pastor listened and put on his eyeglasses in order to hear better.

"Upon my soul, so there is! Who can it—who can it be, I wonder?"

"Get up and go outside and see!" the wife answered, giving her old man another jab in the ribs.

The Pastor hurriedly put on his heavy woolen drawers and his fur coat, pushed his feet into a pair of overshoes, took down his shotgun from the wall, put on a hat and put in a cartridge, shook down the priming powder, and went outside.

"Hey, there! Who is there?" he called out.

"Flod!" answered a dull, tired voice from behind the lilac bushes.

"What the devil can be wrong that you've come all the way here at this hour of the night? Your old mother isn't lying on her deathbed, is she?"

"No, it's something much worse what's happened to her," Gusten said, showing exhaustion, his voice almost at the breaking point. "We lost her!"

"You lost her? . . ."

"Yes—we lost her—in the sea!"

"But for God's sake, come on in and let's not stand out here in this freezing weather."

When Gusten came inside and stood in the light, he looked like a blown-out egg, for he had neither eaten nor drunk anything the whole day, and had had besides the awful and depleting experience of trying to win a battle not only against sea and snow, sleet and ice, but against the east wind, which he had succeeded in outracing.

After Gusten, who scarcely stopped to take a breath, had related to Pastor Nordström how it had all happened, the Pastor went to ask his wife for the key to a certain cupboard in the kitchen. This led to a brief tempest, but after a few minutes the Pastor was in possession of the treasured key and led his shipwrecked visitor into the kitchen. There he seated

Gusten at the big kitchen table and placed before his famished guest strong Swedish brandy, lardbutter, head-cheese, and bread.

Then the two talked over what might be done for Gusten's missing companions. To go out at this hour of the night and in the dense darkness, trying to summon together rescuers, would be a useless effort; and to build bonfires on the shore was always risky, as the flames might deceive and lead astray seafarers who sighted them through the fog and the blizzard.

Gusten and the Pastor thought the men who had saved themselves on the rocky islet were not in any immediate danger. On the other hand, Carlsson's fate gave cause for grave concern. Gusten seemed to be convinced that the ice had broken up in the cove and that by this time there was little hope that his step-father might have survived. And he ended by saying that it looked to him "as if Carlsson had been given his just deserts for his evil deeds in the past."

"Now, Gusten, listen to me!" Pastor Nordström remonstrated. "It seems to me that you have all been judging Carlsson unjustly. And when you talk about his evil deeds, I don't know what you mean. What condition was the farm in when he came and took hold of it, eh? Hasn't he worked up the homestead for you since he came? Didn't he procure tenants for the summer months for you, and didn't he build a new house? That he married Flod's widow—well, she was anxious to get him, wasn't she? And that he asked her to make her will in his favor—you can't blame him for trying; but it was certainly injudicious of her to sign it. Carlsson was a smart, nimble fellow, and he did what you would have liked to do but couldn't and didn't! Am I not right? —Didn't you want me to speak about marriage for you to the widow over at Åvassa, with her eight thousand in the bank, didn't you? No, no, Gusten, you should not be so severe in your judgment of people! And you must learn to realize that every man has a right to his own opinions."

"Well, you may be right, Pastor—but if it hadn't been for him, my mother wouldn't be dead now! And that's something I ain't going to forget soon!"

"Oh, don't talk nonsense! The moment you creep into bed with your wife, you will have forgotten all about it! And besides—who knows whether he was actually responsible for her death? If your mother, for instance, had put some warm clothes on that night before running out in the bitter cold, she might still be alive. And I can't believe she could have been so terribly upset because he—a young fellow—had a little fiddle-faddle with a young girl. But now the whole matter seems to have come to an end, and tomorrow morning we'll have to see what we can do. Tomorrow is Sunday, and then, I presume, the people will be coming to church, and so we won't have to call on them at their homes to get them together. And now— go to bed, Gusten, and take it easy; and remember what the old proverb says: "The death of one man means bread and butter for another.""

On the following morning, when the folk who had come to attend the Sunday service were standing on the slope in front of the church, Pastor Nordström came marching up, accompanied by Gusten Flod. Instead of entering the church, he stopped and talked with the men—who seemed to have already heard rumors about what had happened. After the parson announced that no church service would be held that Sunday, he urged them all to gather at the church pier with their boats without delay, and to go to the aid of the men in distress. There were some who grumbled at going, the pretext being that they hated to miss the divine message, but these murmurings came from a scattered few in the back of the crowd, who bore a grudge against Carlsson, partly because he came from the mainland, and partly because of his aggressiveness at community council meetings.

"Stop your nonsense!" the Pastor retorted. "You are

not so terribly keen about listening to my watery Sunday sermons and admonitions, if I know you aright! Eh? Or what do you say, Åvassa—you who are so familiar with the scriptures that you know them almost by heart and can tell the moment I come to the bottom of the soap barrel?"

The Pastor's sarcasm was greeted by the congregation with quiet laughter, and all opposition came to an end.

"Anyhow, there'll be another Sunday coming next week! Come to church then, and I promise you, I'll make up for today—I'll put the heat on good, you'll see! And be sure to bring your womenfolk along with you, and I'll give them a raking over, too, that'll last them for at least seven weeks! Well—are we going to get the ass out of the pit, or aren't we?"*

"Yes! Yes! We are ready!" shouted the group in unison, as if they had been given mass absolution for not resting on this sabbath.

Then the crowd scattered, and each one went to his home to change clothes and get ready to set out in the boats.

The blizzard had come to an end, the wind had swung around to the north, and the weather was cold and clear. The cove was in perpetual motion, the surging sea breaking in bluish-black colors against the snow-white, gleaming island rocks, when ten or more fishing-boats put out from the church pier. The men had put on heavy fur coats and sealskin caps and had taken along axes, dragrope, and grappling iron. To think of using sails was out of the question, and so they manned the oars. The Pastor sat with Gusten in the first boat, which was rowed by four crack fisher-

* "Which of you shall have an ass or an ox fallen into a pit, and will not straightway pull him out on the sabbath day?" Luke 14:5.—A.P.

men and seamen from the skerries; and Boatswain Rapp acted as lookout and bow-oar.*

Everyone was in a serious mood, but no one was excessively grave or disconsolate; one human life more or less, lost to the sea, could not be dwelt on too dolefully.

A fairly heavy sea was running, and the water that was washed aboard froze at once and had to be broken up and tossed back into the sea. Now and then an icefloe drifted toward them, scraping against the outer planking, diving under and coming up again, sometimes with leaves, frozen reeds, and pieces of twig clinging to it after they had been torn loose from the shore.

Pastor Nordström sat looking in the direction of Trälskär through his binoculars. It was there the men from Hemsö were marooned. Now and then he cast a hopeless look over the cove, where Carlsson had unquestionably met his death in the deep; then again his eyes searched for some sort of clue on the drifting icefloes—the imprint of a foot, a piece of clothing, or the man's dead body. But there was no sign of anything anywhere.

After having rowed a couple of hours, they were within sight of the little island. Rundquist and Norman had observed the approaching rescue flotilla some distance away, and out of joy had lit bonfires on the shore; and when the boats put to at the rocky shore, they showed not so much emotion as curiosity, for their lives had not been in any danger.

"There ain't never no danger so long as you got dry land under your feet," Rundquist expostulated.

As there was not much time left before the light would begin to wane, the salvaging of the foundered Hemsö boat began immediately; and when that task

* With the duty of fending off with a boathook upon landing.—A.P.

was completed, they began dragging for the lost coffin and corpse.

Rundquist was able to prognosticate, he said, the exact spot where old Mrs. Carlsson's body lay buried, because he had seen luminescent fire rising up out of the sea. The spot was dragged over and over again, but the only thing they hooked was interminable lengths of seaweed, in which mussels and other crawling things of the sea were entangled. The dragging went on all morning and continued until late into the afternoon. The men began to look tired and disheartened. Some of them had gone ashore to get a nip of liquor and a sandwich, or to make themselves a cup of coffee; and then Gusten finally concluded that it would be useless to continue the search since the current had by this time most probably carried the coffin out into the depths of the sea.

As none of the men were especially eager to see the dead woman come floating into sight, and the matter, strictly speaking, was of no personal concern to anyone but Gusten, they all felt a certain measure of relief at not having to show themselves to be unfeeling in the face of another's grief and mourning.

However, in order to give a final touch of respectability to an ignominious and sorry ending, Pastor Nordström came up to Flod and asked if he would not like him to say a few words as a memorial to his dead mother. The parson had brought the Book with him, and he supposed that the men knew at least one hymn by heart. Gusten gratefully accepted the parson's offer, and the fugitive little island congregation was summoned and told of the service.

The sun was about to descend beyond the horizon after having ended its brief daytime visit, and the skerries lay rosy-red, bathing themselves in its last diminishing rays of light, as the men grouped together on the shore to join in the improvised burial ceremony, adapted to the circumstances.

The Pastor stepped down into one of the boats, and Gusten went with him. The Pastor went to the stern, took out his book, held his handkerchief between his left-hand fingers, and bared his head; and the men on the shore removed their caps.

"Let us take number 432: 'Toward death I go'! You know it by heart—all of you?" the Pastor asked.

"Yes—we do!" was the answer from the congregation on the shore.

The singing of the hymn began, rising from voices which at first quivered from the freezing atmosphere but soon after from emotion, engendered by the stark simplicity and the unusualness of the ceremony and the moving strains of the old psalm which had accompanied so many to their final sleep of peace.

The last tones had rung out and were echoing far away over the water, against rocks and skerries, through the chill air, and there was a pause, during which they could hear only the sighing and soughing of the northwind in the needle-foliage of the dwarfed pine trees, the plashing of the waves between the boulders, the cries of the sea gulls, and the bumping of the boats against the offshore sea bottom.

The Pastor turned his old, furrowed face and gazed out toward the cove, and the sun shone upon his bald head, about which gray wisps of hair were fluttering in the wind like hanging lichen on an aged spruce tree.

"Earth to earth, ashes to ashes, dust to dust, in sure and certain hope of the Resurrection to eternal life, through Jesus Christ our Lord. Let us pray," he began in a deep voice that had to battle with wind and waves to make itself heard.

And so the burial ceremony continued until he had read the Lord's Prayer; and after having given the blessing, he stretched out his hand over the water in a final farewell.

The men put on their caps again. Gusten pressed

Pastor Nordström's hand and thanked him, but there seemed to be something on his mind that he wanted to give voice to.

"Pastor Nordström—I thought that . . . Don't you think you ought to have said a word for Carlsson, too?"

"The service was for two, my boy! But it was kind and generous of you to think of him," the old man replied, being more moved than he wanted to show.

The sun went down, and nothing remained for the men to do but to take leave and try to get home as soon as they could.

But before doing so, they wanted to give Gusten Flod a proof of their respect for him; and when the goodbyes had been said and all were seated in their boats, they escorted him part of the way home. Then they lined up their boats as fishermen do when they set their nets, raised their oars in a salute, and shouted: Goodbye!

It was a mark of their sympathy for him in his grief, but also of their sympathy for the young man himself, whom they now accepted as belonging to the ranks of responsible and independent men.

And sitting at the tiller of his own boat, the new master of Hemsö had his farmhands row him homeward. From now on he was the master also of his own ship of fortune on the stormy coves and greening inlets of the fickle Sea of Life.